"It's very rare that a new author writes such a great book that is a keeper . . ."
Romance in Color, 4 stars

"Niobia Bryant is off to a good start . . . a very strong three heart read . . . added to my Emerging Author's list"
Gwenn Osborne, Romance Reader, 3 of 4 hearts

"A well-crafted story with engaging secondary characters."
Affaire de Coeur, 4½ stars,—ADMISSION OF LOVE

". . . this sneaky little romance heats up gradually, then sizzles until done . . ."
Doubleday's Black Expression Book Club Review—THREE TIMES A LADY

". . . a refreshing read with wonderful characters and a "true family". A wonderful TOP PICK for the month of June!"
Romantic Times, 4½ stars, TOP PICK—THREE TIMES A LADY

"*Heavenly Match* is a wonderfully romantic story with an air of mystery and suspense that draws the reader in, encouraging them to put aside everything and everyone until they have read the book in its entirety."
RAWSistaz Review, 4 stars

"'Sexy as sin' describes this provocative novel to a T."
Romantic Times Magazine, 4½ stars, TOP PICK—CAN'T GET NEXT TO YOU

"This is a great story. There is humor, sensuality, and just great chemistry between the two main characters. . . . So check out this funny and sexy romance story because Niobia Bryant has written a gem."
Imani Book Club, 4 out of 5—CAN'T GET NEXT TO YOU

"Run to the bookstore and pick up this delightful read. This reunion story is touching, warm, sensuous, and at times, sad. But just try to put Bryant's book down."
Romantic Times Magazine, 4½ stars, TOP PICK—Let's Do it Again

Heated

Niobia Bryant

Kensington Publishing Corp.
http://www.kensingtonbooks.com

DAFINA BOOKS are published by

Kensington Publishing Corp.
850 Third Avenue
New York, NY 10022

All Kensington Titles, Imprints, and Distributed Lines are available at special quantity discounts for bulk purchases for sales
promotions, premiums, fund-raising, and educational or insti-
tutional use. Special book excerpts or customized printings can
also be created to fit specific needs. For details, write or phone
the office of the Kensington special sales manager: Kensington
Publishing Corp., 850 Third Avenue, New York, NY 10022,
attn: Special Sales Department, Phone: 1-800-221-2647.

Dafina and the Dafina logo Reg. U.S. Pat. & TM Off.

First Dafina mass market printing: June 2006

10 9 8 7 6 5 4 3 2 1

Printed in the United States of America

For the one who keeps me heated:
Tony Holmes

Acknowledgments

To my family and friends, thanks for any and all support and love you have given me over the years.

To my editor, Karen Thomas, and her assistant, Nicole Bruce, thanks for all the hard work you put into this project.

To my agent, Claudia, thanks for being one of the best at doing what you do.

To my sistah in the word and fellow Sagittarian, Adrianne Byrd, thank you for all the industry info and for being someone I can always be "real" with.

To the wonderful network of African-American bookstores and book clubs, thank you for keeping me and so many other African-American writers going with your invaluable support.

To my readers, whom I cherish, thank you for wanting to experience each and every one of my books. You all are the reason I nearly *live* in my office—smile.

To the wonderful members of my book club, Niobia Bryant News, thank you for making me strive to make sure each project is better than the last.

Love 2 Live & Live 2 Love,

N.

Prologue

Careful not to alert anyone to his presence, he moved in the darkness across the wild and grassy field with speed. He was nervous that he would be caught before his mission was complete. Like thunder and drums all rolled into one, his heart pounded in his chest. Sweat dampened his shirt, making it cling to his shoulders and back.

A sudden noise echoed from the surrounding darkness. He caught his breath and held it as nerves caused his bladder to fill. He quickly dropped down, pressing his stomach and knees to the cool earth surrounded by weeds and grass that was nearly three to four feet tall.

Holding his breath . . . he waited. Listening. Scared of being caught.

He heard nothing but the normal night sounds of the country: owls hooting, frogs singing their tunes, crickets busy scratching their legs.

Warily, he rose and moved ahead.

When the barn—already worn and torn from age and shameful neglect—came into view, he paused. For a second he looked up at the massive structure framed by the full moonlight.

It was almost majestic.

Swallowing any regret, he dashed inside.

He emerged moments later and ran as quickly as he could away from it. His feet thudded against the earth, his chest heaved with pain from his exertion.

He dared turning around only when he was cloaked by the trees—trees that welcomed and hid him.

The flames engulfing the barn were reflected in his ebony eyes.

1

"Say cheese, Dr. King."

Bianca smiled as instructed, posing with her glass star-shaped Woman of the Year award from *Modern Women* magazine held in front of her. She tried not to grimace as the flash went off several times in rapid succession.

"Absolutely beautiful, Bianca."

Her smile stiffened. She knew without shifting her eyes from the camera that it was Armand Toussaint.

"Thanks, Dr. King and congrats again," the male photographer said, moving back into the Imperial Ballroom of the Marriott Marquis Hotel to take further photos of the social event.

Bianca took a deep breath as she slid her circle-shaped beaded purse under her arm. She had just stepped into the hall outside the ballroom for a small reprieve from the room of people there to honor her with yet another accomplishment in her career as an equine veterinarian.

She considered Armand's appearance an intrusion.

"Hello, Armand," she said, not even sounding like she meant it.

"*Une belle femme ne doit pas être seule*," he said, his French accent very heavy as he told her she was too beautiful to be alone.

Armand had lived around the world and spoke seven languages, but when he was really trying to put his mack down he always reverted to French—a language he knew Bianca spoke fluently.

Bianca sighed. "I thank you for the compliment on my beauty, but I also thank you for respecting my desire to be alone," she countered with ease. She knew it would take more bluntness to send the amorous admirer truly on his way.

It's not like he wasn't appealing to the eye—the man was tall and gorgeous like a young Sidney Poitier—and Bianca even found his conversation quite amusing—when he wasn't trying to seduce her out of her La Perla panties . . . and there was a certain allure to a tall man with skin like dark chocolate with a French accent. The man was just insufferable because he was aware of his attributes and he couldn't fathom that there was a woman in existence who didn't want him.

Bianca certainly didn't.

She usually ran into Armand at the many charity and social events they attended in Atlanta. They both served on several of the same boards, advisory councils, and minority organizations. On every occasion—whether with a date or not—Armand let Bianca know that he had a personal cure for her "supposed" loneliness blues.

Was Bianca lonely?

She fixed her hazel eyes on the rogue and saw his eyes shift to her left. Bianca turned to see what drew his attention and her eyes fell on a curvaceous woman in a strapless dress that defied gravity. She turned her gaze back to him and he smiled at her in a charming—and apologetic—fashion.

Not *that* lonely.

She firmly believed his penis had more miles on it than two hundred laps around the Indianapolis Speedway. Even though he loved to tell Bianca that he was quite skilled in making a woman come at least ten times in one session of lovemaking, Bianca was more than willing to pass.

"No one should be alone on such a beautiful night as tonight, *mon doux*," he said in a husky voice, stepping closer to her.

Bianca stepped back. "I'm sure you'll find . . . *something* to get into," she told him wryly.

"Bianca—"

Her cell phone rang from inside her purse. "Excuse me, Armand," she told him, pulling it out to answer. "Dr. King speaking."

"This is Travis out at the Clover Ranch."

"Yes, hello Travis."

"We got a mare about to foal. We've been monitoring her and she was doing good with the rolling to position the foal, but for the last five minute she's actin' awful funny for normal foaling, you know?"

Bianca nodded. "Has her water broke?"

"No, ma'am."

"I'm about twenty good minutes from the ranch, but I'm on my way."

"Thank God," Travis sighed.

Bianca bit back a smile before she ended the call.

Armand came to stand beside her, lightly touching her bare elbow. "Everything okay, Bianca?"

"I have to go. Please make my apologies to everyone."

"But—"

"Goodbye, Armand."

Bianca flew out of the ballroom, not even waiting for the elevator as she took to the grand staircase. She was quite a site with her shoulder-length pressed hair flying behind her and the slinky skirt of her mocha sequined Roberto Cavali dress in her hands as she hitched it up around her knees to run straight down the center of the staircase.

Very Scarlet O'Hara–like.

She wasn't aware or caring of the dramatic sight she made, though. She just wanted to get to the ranch and it was a good fifteen miles just outside of Atlanta in Sandy Springs.

Thank God I keep a change of clothes in my trunk.

She was soon accepting the keys to her silver convertible Volvo C70. She lowered the automatic roof as she sped away from the hotel.

"Home sweet home."

The sun was just beginning to rise when Bianca dragged herself into the foyer of her elegant three thousand square foot home in an affluent gated community in a suburb of Atlanta. She flung her dress over the banister and carried her award into her study. She came to a stop before her massive cherry desk and took in the full wall of shelves behind it. Every accomplishment of her adult life was chronicled. There were more awards and accolades than she could count. She didn't even know if she could make room for her latest achievement.

Reflective, she walked to the far end of the study and slowly began to review all of the statues in various shapes, sizes, and materials. Some meant more to her than others, and those she touched briefly with a hint of a smile.

For anyone on the outside looking in at her life it was seemingly ideal.

She started her own veterinary practice at twenty-seven from her savings. Just three short years later her workload nearly doubled and she brought on two additional vets. She was now thirty-two, and her equine clinic was one of the top such facilities in the Southeast.

Not bad for a little black girl from Holtsville, South Carolina.

Bianca came to a stop before the 8 × 11 photograph in the center of the wall of awards and certifications. It was a picture of a tall and distinguished man standing beside a little girl and woman atop a horse. They were all smiling and obviously happy.

My eighth birthday, Bianca thought.

Her parents had just surprised her with her very first pony, Star. Even though she had had plenty access to ponies living on a successful horse ranch Star had been special because it was hers alone.

The photo was one of the few that she treasured.

A reminder of better times.

The little girl in that picture didn't have a clue that her mother would die seven years later and her stable world would never be the same again.

Bianca set her award on the shelf with the photo as her eyes fell on the handsome man. Her father. Her Daddy. Once her hero.

She hadn't seen him or the ranch in fifteen years.

When her mother died Bianca thought her world would end. Her one saving grace had been her close relationship with her father. She knew they would help each other through the loss.

But that hadn't happened.

Her father shut down completely. He isolated himself in his bedroom for days at a time, only to emerge reeking of alcohol. The ranch felt his neglect, right along with Bianca. That hurt.

It was far too much weight for a fifteen year old to bear. Between going to school—and maintaining her grades—and trying to take over running the farm, she would sometimes wake up and find her father sprawled out by the door drunk as a skunk.

She barely had time to grieve her mother's passing because she began cleaning up her father's messes. She became really good at it. She became just as good at hiding her anger and disappointment.

Until the day her father brought home Trishon Haddock—a woman twenty years his junior—and proclaimed that at forty he was getting married.

That's when Bianca—soft, agreeable, and passive—welcomed that part of her personality that let her hit the roof. It hadn't been little Bianca struggling to make sense of her world. She was seventeen-year-old Bianca, senior in high school, and running a horse ranch—and she was *pissed*.

Even though she told her father that he was being a fool for marrying a woman with the reputation around town of a harlot; even though she told him he was disrespecting her and her Mama by bringing another woman into their house; even though she refused to be nice as he requested . . . she never once told him that it hurt her that he made time in his life for a wife when he hadn't made time for his daughter.

That she held on to, protected, shielded.

As she stood at her second-story bedroom window and looked down at the wedding she refused to attend,

Bianca made the decision to leave her father in the chaos *he* created. Bianca rescinded her decision to attend a local university. The further she got away, the better.

She left for college in Georgia that summer and hadn't been back since.

Bianca turned away from the photo, but her memories— very painful recollections—remained. Her relationship with her father was barely visible. They spoke on the phone sporadically and went through motions.

Pathetic as hell, she thought.

Releasing a heavy breath, Bianca strolled out of the study and headed toward the rear of the house to her kitchen. She was ready to fall into her bed and sleep away the hours, but she had appointments at the clinic, so rest would have to wait.

Bianca hoped some of her "kick-ass" iced coffee would get her going again.

Soon the slow drip-drip of the coffee maker seemed to be the only sound in the house. Most considered that quiet to be peaceful, restful, and precious. To Bianca it was the sound of living alone, which she refused to equate to being lonely. Sometimes, however, she thought that the sound of children laughing and a husband showering to prepare for his workday would be . . . peaceful, restful, and precious.

With her last date being more than two months ago perhaps the line between alone and lonely was thinning to the width of a strand of hair.

"Maybe I need a dog," she muttered, pouring a large cup of coffee that she sweetened and lightened considerably before pouring it over a tall cup of crushed ice.

Bianca took a deep sip. "Liquid crack," she sighed.

She was strolling out of the kitchen when there was a knock at her kitchen door. She smiled at the sight of her nearest neighbor and friend, Mimi Cooley, peering through the glass of the door.

"Let me in, Sweetie, before people think I'm a Peeping Tom, okay," Mimi said in that odd voice of hers that was a blend of nasal whining and Southern belle haughtiness.

Mimi was an ex–child star of the popular Seventies sitcom, *Just the Two of Us*. At thirteen, the show was canceled and, unfortunately, her acting career ended. Her family moved from Hollywood back to Atlanta and tried to give Mimi as normal a life as possible.

But normalcy and Mimi didn't go in the same sentence.

She married the first of her seven husbands at eighteen—men who were wealthy and a tad bit older than Mimi. At fifty she now lived off syndication from the show and the hundreds of television commercials she did during her childhood career. She never got used to the idea of a nine to five job, and spent her days shopping and drinking Long Island iced teas—without showing one indication of being drunk or even tipsy.

Regardless of the time of day, Mimi was always dressed to the nines: heels and skirts, slacks and spectator pumps, and not a pair of jeans to be seen. Her make-up was always in place, and her hair was perfectly coiffed—and religiously died jet black—like she was the second coming of Diahann Carroll's character on *Dynasty*.

Mimi was one of a kind, and Bianca loved the diva to death.

"Hi, Mimi."

She breezed in with a cloud of Chanel No. 5 and turquoise silk. "I thought I was going to have to retire and collect Social Security before you let me in, darling."

"How can I help you, Mimi . . . *dah-ling*?"

"Well, a shot of brandy wouldn't hurt a bit, Sweetie,"

Mimi said, moving across the kitchen to set her purse on the center island.

"For 8 A.M. coffee sounds like a better bet," Bianca countered.

"Some barkeep you make. All that advice without the actual, huh, what . . . liquor, that's right, Sweetie."

"Nothing but coffee 'round here," Bianca said, taking a deep sip of her iced brew. "Want a cup?"

Mimi rolled her elaborately made-up eyes—she was so dramatic. "Sweetie, I'd rather be buried in a Wal-Mart, okay," she said with a shiver.

Bianca doubted Mimi had even seen the inside of a Wal-Mart, or even knew where to find one. She frowned as she watched Mimi open her purse and extract a silver monogrammed flask.

"Bianca, a lady is always, huh, what . . . prepared, that's right," she said, before taking a small swig. "Now, I usually have the cul de sac all to myself this time of day. Whatcha doing home, Sweetie?"

"A mare foaled last night."

Mimi wiped the corners of her mouth with her index finger and politely placed the flask back in her purse. "Honey, I'm waiting for the English translation, okay, right."

Bianca smiled as she folded her arms over her chest and leaned back against the marble counter. "I delivered a horse's baby," she explained patiently, ready for the drama. Mimi didn't fail her one bit.

She made a comical face of pain as she pressed her knees together.

Mimi didn't have any children. Bianca didn't know if it was by choice or not.

Deciding to egg her on Bianca said, "Pulling the foal out with chains by its legs wasn't the hard part—"

Mimi shivered and crossed her slender legs.

"Now sticking my arm inside the horse's vagina to turn the foal—"

Mimi pretended to gag. "T.M.I., Doc. T . . . M . . . I."

Bianca flung her head back and laughed, unable to stop the hoglike snort that always came with her laughter. T.M.I. was Mimi's acronym, for "too much information."

"I don't know what's worse, Sweetie. The image of your arm up a horse's ass or that laugh, Sweetie. You need to, huh, what . . . work on it, that's right."

"Shut up, Mimi," Bianca said with a deadpan expression. "At least I'm not known for the oh-so-clever sitcom saying "You and me makes we.""

Mimi looked off into the distance—something she did whenever she was discussing the sitcom. "Oh, yes. A better time. And it kept me from being lined up to swallow the scent of horse ass, Sweetie."

Bianca had to laugh at that one. "Listen, this is fun, but some people got a job, Mimi."

She rose, sticking her purse under her arm. "Alright, Sweetie, I'm going. I have a save the children or feed the whales breakfast thingy."

"Isn't it Save the Whales and Feed the Children?"

Mimi just waved her hand before moving to the kitchen door. "As long as they can cash the check, they don't care what I call it."

Bianca shook her head.

Mimi opened the door and paused, turning to look at Bianca. "Listen, Sweetie, is what they say about a male horse's . . . uhm, well, you know . . . jingy-thingy. Is that . . . is that true, Sweetie?"

Very tongue in cheek, Bianca answered, "Big as my arm," with a meaningful stare.

Mimi sighed as she patted her perfectly coiffed

French roll and leaned a little against the door with a soft smile.

"Mimi?" Bianca said to nudge the woman out of her reverie.

"Just made me think of Vincent, my third husband, Sweetie. Now it's so hard to say *he* was good for nothing."

With nothing to say about *that*, Bianca started walking out the kitchen. "Goodbye, Mimi," she called over her shoulder.

"Toodles, Sweetie."

The door closed behind her.

Bianca climbed the spiral wrought iron staircase to the second level of her home. As she strolled into her master suite she looked at her watch. It was 9:30 A.M. Just enough time to shower, change, and head to her clinic for a 10:30 A.M. appointment. Her next appointment after that was at 1 P.M., and she was hoping to visit Mr. Sandman as much as she could before then.

Bianca removed the scrubs she kept in her car for emergency vet calls like last night. Dressed only in the beautiful lace thong she originally put on under her evening gown, Bianca took another deep sip of her drink as she moved over to her night table to check her messages. She had a service answer work-related calls and she'd already checked those messages during her drive from Sandy Springs.

"Hi, this is Bianca. Do what you need to do."

Beep.

Bianca studied her reflection in the oval mirror in the corner, twisting and turning to see if any new cellulite had moved onto her thighs.

"Bunny . . . uh, I mean Bianca—"

She paused at the sound of her father's gravely and

distinctive voice. The thought that the days of him calling her by the childhood pet name were gone pained her.

"Call me when you get a chance."

Bianca lowered her hands from examining the pertness of her breasts—and wondering when a man would touch, tease, and taste them again—to reach out for the cordless phone sitting on its base.

Beep.

"Bianca—"

Her hand paused just above the phone and her face became confused at hearing her father's voice . . . again.

"Never mind."

The line went dead.

Beep.

Snatching up the phone she quickly dialed her father's number.

"King Ranch."

"Daddy, this is Bianca. Is something wrong?" she asked.

He remained quiet—and that was more telling than anything he could have said.

"Daddy?" she asked with more firmness in her voice—like she was the parent and he was the child. Bianca pressed the phone closer to her face. "What is it?"

"I need your help. You gotta come home, Bianca."

2

Holtsville, SC
One week later

Being in Holtsville was like going back in time for
Bianca. Virtually nothing had changed. Even Donnie's
Diner remained the only eatery in the small "downtown"
area—thank the heavens it was renovated. Donnie's was
a landmark in Holtsville, but growing up she felt eating
from there was like playing Russian Roulette with your
digestive system.

Yes, Holtsville was still a one gas station town. As she
passed by it, Bianca waved at the grizzly man sweeping
in front of the storefront. She smiled as she remembered
riding with her father to the small store, anxious to spend
her nickels and pennies on candy.

Good memories.

Bianca pushed her oversized shades up atop her mass
of straw set curls as she turned left off the main road. Her
father's ranch was on sixty acres, just ten miles away. As
she drove, Bianca looked around at the small houses that

looked the same as when she growing up. Many of her childhood memories were tied to those places.

Cutting the models from the Sears catalogs to play with like paper dolls on the porch of her best friend, Patty Ann. Or her first kiss at the Walker property with Lil' Willie Walker up in the loft of his family's barn.

Bianca laughed as she remembered screaming and running from the barn when he whipped out *his* little Willie.

Lots of memories.

Now she was back in town.

Last week when her father asked for her to come home, Bianca had reservations, but she set them aside. She knew it took quite a feat for *her* father to ask for help. For him to admit that he was close to losing the ranch was astounding. For him to say he *needed* her was the clincher.

"Well, can you beat that?" Bianca said aloud, her eyes lighting on the wooden sign that read:

KING EQUINE SERVICES
ESTABLISHED 1959
HOLTSVILLE, SC
(2 MILES AHEAD ON RIGHT)

She clearly remembered the day she helped her father hang the sign that her mother painted with care. And there it remained after all that time. The letters were faded and the corners of the wood was chipped, but her father hadn't replaced it.

Maybe this trip won't be so bad after all.

Bianca noticed a large and shiny pick-up truck behind her in her rearview mirror. She paid it no mind until the driver began to blow the truck's horn and motion out the window with his hand.

Bianca checked her speedometer. She was doing fifty-five. *Humph.* "Better go around," she muttered with attitude.

As the truck passed, Bianca noticed a man wearing aviator shades and riding in the back. The man and his pose looked straight out of one of those Ralph Lauren print ads—even done to the chocolate lab sitting dutifully at his side.

The man made Bianca want to do something naughty, like suck her finger or blow him kisses.

Ruggedly handsome, his salt and pepper smooth hair was cut very low. His beard and mustache was more a five o'clock shadow. She knew his hair was prematurely silver because there was no denying the youth and vitality of the man. She figured him to be in his early thirties, and his deep bronzed caramel complexion perfectly suited that beautiful hair. He had strong features. A lighter version of that male supermodel, Tyson.

Bianca wished his shades weren't in place.

Her eyes took in the black tank he wore and the way it snugly fit his chest and emphasized the steely muscles of his arms.

Just before the truck accelerated and left her behind, the man waved at her before setting his arm atop his bent knee. The move drew her attention to the large tattoo of an eagle on his upper right arm.

"Ooh, come here, you," she said to herself, waving back with a beguiling smile and a little toot-toot of her horn.

Good girls *always* loved bad boys, and there was something untamed and wicked about the man that drew her in. "Sexy silver self," she said in a low voice to herself.

Did he like what he saw as well? She couldn't help but get excited at the thought that he did.

Moments later the truck became a spot in the distance.

"Whew, he was fine," Bianca moaned, just as she decelerated the car to turn it down the long and winding dirt road leading to the ranch.

The grove of trees lining the road offered enough shade to make one think it was suddenly late evening and not early afternoon. As a child Bianca would play among that blanket of trees, feeling like a princess in her own secret garden. Even when it rained the tree's branches were so densely intertwined that nary a raindrop broke through to touch the ground.

Then the trees ended. Before her sat her childhood home, the King's Castle as her father used to call it. The two-story home was an impressive structure. A huge wrap-around porch and so many windows that the sun glinting off the glass looked like the twinkle of diamonds. The navy blue shutters crisply contrasted off the white of the home with the underskirt of the home trimmed in red brick.

The mahogany front door opened and her father stepped out onto the porch, his arms already opened wide. Bianca flew out of the car and ran up the stairs to him. He enveloped her. She clung to his large impressive frame and to a past when there was no distance between them.

Although Bianca hadn't returned once since she left college.

Although she owned a house in Atlanta just as large as this.

Although she swore to never return if things hadn't changed.

Her first thoughts were, *I'm home*.

* * *

As Kahron Strong stood in the doorway of his bed-room and looked at the naked woman lying there like she was posing for *Playboy*, he wondered who he'd have to pay to get a housekeeper on whom he could rely.

This woman laying before was Erika—the fifteenth housekeeper/cook he hired since he moved to Holtsville, SC. He tried everything from the old to the young, male, female, and a few that could swing either way. He always got the same result—they did *something* to get on his last nerve.

Whether it was stealing, or being disrespectful, or watching more of his digital cable than actually working, or foolishly trying to seduce him—Erika was the fourth such to try that route—or just plain couldn't cook or clean to save their lives, Kahron went through housekeep-ers quicker than tissue. He wondered if he was cursed.

Because she was laying out the goods he gave her a quick perusal. He shook his head. When a man has a naked woman lying before him and he notices that the furry mound between her legs is starting to grow *down* her legs—well, something just wasn't right.

"Ma'am, please go on and get dressed," he said, his voice raspy and filled with his Down South accent. He reached into his back pocket and pulled two twenty-dollar bills off the knot of money. "Your services are no longer needed."

"What?" she exclaimed, actually opening her legs wider.

Kahron diverted his gaze and tried not to laugh at how ridiculous she was.

"Are you crazy?" she asked.

"No, ma'am."

"You *ain't* all that, Kahron Strong."

"Yes, ma'am, I know."

He heard the rustle of the sheets and the squeal of the bed springs as she rose. He started to tell her to take the sheets with her, but refrained—he'd just throw them out. He felt sheets were almost as intimate as underwear and, well, it just wasn't something he wanted to randomly share.

Kahron looked at wall until she snatched the money from his hand and slammed out of the room.

"Well, another one bites the dust," he said, as the front door slammed soon after.

After a long day at the livestock auction in Chesnee, Kahron had just wanted to eat lunch and help his crew out with repairing the fence on the northeast portion of his one hundred acre spread.

A strip show hadn't been on his "to do" list—especially from a woman whose crotch looked like she had Buckwheat's head trapped between her legs.

He made himself a cheese sandwich—there weren't any cold cuts in sight—before heading back out of the house. His dog, a chocolate lab aptly name Hershey, immediately rose from where she was lazily lounging on her favorite spot on the porch. Kahron paused to give Hershey the rest of his sandwich and he stroked her coat as she lapped it up with ease.

"Good girl," he said, with one last pat to her side.

Kahron could have driven one of the four battered work trucks or three four wheelers parked in front of his single-level house, but he decided to ride his stallion, Midnight, instead. With Hershey at his booted heels, he walked the distance over to the steel barn that housed his ten horses.

"*Hola* Paco," Kahron greeted the ten year old as he

walked up. Paco was the son of Kahron's stable manager, Carlos Santos.

"*Hola* Mister Strong."

Kahron mussed his wild cap of black hair playfully, quite fond of the child. "Will you get Midnight for me?"

Paco didn't even bother to answer. He just dashed off to do as he was asked.

As he waited, Kahron looked around at all the activity on his ranch. He loved it. All of the ranch hands within his sight were busy with a task, be it shoeing a horse or cleaning up the constant animal droppings. Since buying the ranch six years ago, Kahron had improved the water availability and distribution with better grazing management, increased the size of the herd by nearly three hundred heads, and increased the staff to thirty men— twelve of whom resided on the property in the bunkhouse. His goal was to expand further.

The ranch currently dealt mainly with livestock, but Kahron was looking into possibly expanding into dairy, like his brother Kaleb, who farmed in Walterboro just twenty miles away. That would come in due time. Right now his focus was getting ready to drive his herd to the south pasture of his land in a few weeks.

"Here he is, Mister Strong," Paco said, carefully leading the horse to him. "I groomed him for you."

Kahron pulled five dollars from his pocket. "Best brushing job I ever seen, Paco."

The little boy's mouth formed into an circle and he went running off. He stopped after a few feet. "*Gracias*, Mister Strong. Come on Hershey," he shouted back before dashing off to the back of the stable, presumably to find his father.

Hershey, who was particular about what action she chose to partake in, just stood there and watched the little boy run off before she trotted over to her pile of blankets in the corner of the tack room.

"Lazy girl," Kahron teased, as he walked into the tack room to retrieve his custom made black leather saddle.

Hershey just settled deeper into her blankets.

Kahron laughed as he walked back out to Midnight. He grunted slightly as he saddled his horse, stroking the deep ebony of its powerful neck, its mane long, flowing, and just as black. Moments later, comfortably mounted on the horse's back, Kahron went trotting off to help the set of men repairing fence, his thoughts heavy on how ideal the King property would be ideal for expansion of his business.

"Whassup, Bianca."

Bianca stiffened in her father's arms at the sound of her stepmother's voice. Giving her father's wide expanse of body one last hug she step back to look around him at the second Mrs. Hank King . . . Trishon.

Fifteen years later but still young at thirty-five, Trishon was an attractive woman. A bit fuller at the waist, hips, and breasts, but only three years Bianca's senior. Still, she and Trishon had never been close friends growing up. They ran in different circles, but both knew of each other well.

"Hello," Bianca said, barely forcing civility into her tone.

Bianca didn't miss the diamond cluster ring sparkling from the woman's fingers or the casual designer clothing—things Trishon never had until she met and married Hank King.

Kanye West's song "Golddigger" suddenly played in her head.

Trishon's eyes glittered, but she smiled nonetheless. "Hank is so excited about your visit," she said, stepping forward to stand next to him and stroke his arm.

Bianca knew that being a woman would mean giving this woman respect. As much as she hated it, this was Trishon's home—she was the lady of the house—and that meant giving her at least *that* much respect.

"I'm glad to be back, Trishon. Thank you for your hospitality," Bianca said, forcing a smile to her full Angie Stone–like lips.

Bianca looked up at her father, thinking it was good to see his wide handsome face again, and wishing she didn't smell the faint scent of Crown Royal. "I'll have to make you a pot of my homemade stew that you used to love, Daddy."

He smiled. "I would like that."

"I cook for him but he doesn't eat very much," Trishon said, her tone clearly defensive.

Bianca felt irritation nip at her. "We'll just see if both of us can't nag him into eating," she offered lightly.

"Right now I'm headed to run an errand," Hank said, pulling Bianca to his side for another quick hug. "I'll be back later."

Bianca was confused and her face showed it. "But, Daddy, I just got here and don't you think we need to talk?" she asked, even as he continued down the stairs.

"We'll talk when I get back. You and Trishon visit or go shopping or something."

Hank climbed into his battered pick-up truck and Trishon flittered down the stairs behind him.

Bianca watched as he leaned over to pull his wallet out his back pocket and handed some bills into her eager hands.

As he drove away, Bianca felt like that same teenager

whose father ignored her all over again. The first time
he saw his daughter and already he was off with something else—anything else—to do. She released a breath
as if to release the pain and disappointment she felt.

"Trishon, I'm just going to head up to my room,"
Bianca said, jogging down the stairs to pop the trunk of
her vehicle to remove her suitcase.

"Actually, I, uhm, converted your old bedroom into
my dressing room years ago," Trishon said, folding the
money he gave her to push into her brassiere.

"Oh, okay, well, please show me where I'm staying,"
Bianca said through tight lips before climbing the stairs.

"Third room to your right, top of the stairs."

Bianca turned to see Trishon climbing into a red
BMW. The woman said nothing else and just reversed
the car in an arc before accelerating forward in a flurry
of dust.

Disgusted with them both, Bianca entered the house.
She had barely closed the front door behind her, how-
ever, before she froze where she stood. "Sweet Jesus.
What . . . in . . . the . . . *hell*?" she whispered in shock.

Gone was the French country décor that Bianca remembered to be replaced by a design style she could
only name "gaudy chic"—leopard print rugs and throws,
crimson slashes of material that made the room look like
it was bleeding. Leather. Beads. Glass. Metal.

Bianca just rolled her eyes heavenward. Had her
father lost his ever-loving mind? Had she for returning
to this chaos?

She climbed the stairs, her suitcase in her hand, mind-
ful of the changes Trishon made to what was once a
beautiful, classy home. The woman had accomplished
changing it to a remake of The Best Little Whorehouse
in South Carolina. But she was not here to judge, no

matter how bad she thought Trishon' taste was. In two weeks she'd be back in her more . . . *sedate* . . . Atlanta home, living her own life.

Trishon had assigned Bianca to her mother's old sewing room, but any traces of that were gone. It was replaced by every possible shade of purple satin—or was it polyester? Everything from lilac to violet. It looked like the room threw up purple.

She didn't even bother unpacking. She decided to take a look around the ranch because her father wasn't home to give her access to his books. Without even changing out of the vintage jeans, tank, and sneakers she wore, Bianca jogged back downstairs and left the house.

The barn—which was the centerpiece of the business—was a good mile down from the main house. Bianca decided to walk it and headed in that direction. She was anxious to see the horses and meet the ranch hands.

Growing up, King Equine Services had been one of the leading horse ranches for the boarding and breeding of horses in the low country. They used to have a waiting list for people looking to purchase a horse bred and trained by Hank King. He was known for his method of humane and effective training approaches for horses. He seemed to have an affinity for horses, probably through heredity—his own father started the ranch—and through trial and error.

That love of horses and other animals had been passed on to Bianca; thus, her career as a equine vet. She, too, seemed to be blessed with an innate ability with animals. Being a vet gave her the opportunity to make a good deal of money and lots of respect in her field, but she was also surrounded by the horses she loved so much. To her the animals far outweighed the money.

So, it bothered her to think that legacy of quality work and care might be lost. How bad were things? Was it salvageable?

The summer sun was blazing down on her without any shelter from its rays. As she turned down the worn path leading to the area behind the old bunkhouse, Bianca's steps faltered at her first sight of the gable-styled barn—or what was left of it. The structure had not survived what obviously was a fire. What was left was charred, broken, and decrepit. Useless.

Questions flew to mind. The who, what, when, and why of it all.

As she stood in the center of that great field, the tips of the grass dried and yellowing from the heat, Bianca looked around. Not a soul was in sight: the horse pens were empty, no one using the handling chutes to safely contain a horse while trimming feet or treating injuries, no hands walking the horses that should've been boarded, the obstacle courses were desolate.

Uh-oh.

Things were bad. Worst than she thought. If her father didn't get his behind home ASAP she would hunt him down and drag his butt home to explain to her to just what the hell was—or wasn't—going on.

Kahron steered his truck down the long, winding dirt road leading to King Equine Services. Night had fallen and he was hoping Hank was at home so they could talk. That would save him a trip to Charlie's, a small wooden shack at the end of a dead-end road whose namesake sold beer and liquor and allowed the local men to play cards—for a cut. Charlie's was located on the other side of Holtsville, nearer to Summerville, whereas the section of Holtsville he lived in was nearer to Walterboro. Kahron really wasn't up for the drive or the socializing tonight.

His truck had just passed the grove of trees that made that stretch of the road seemed black as midnight when he caught sight of the house. He saw a figure on the porch rise as he neared.

"Well, I'll be damned," he thought with a roguish grin.

It was the curly haired beauty he saw in the convertible earlier today. She looked even better standing.

Hank had bragged that his daughter was coming home, but never had Kahron imagined her to be so beautiful. Guess he was picturing a female version of Hank—which wouldn't have been a pretty sight for anybody's eyes!

She was tall and shapely, something clearly defined by the form fitting jeans and tank that she wore. From her straight up stance he knew she was comfortable in her skin, something that made her even sexier to him. Her reddish-brown hair—he didn't know what else to call it—was the perfect compliment to her light complexion. Her features were feline, with wide eyes and high cheekbones. She had the fullest lips he'd ever seen, and the small mole over her left eyebrow made her all the more endearing.

Kahron was intrigued by her. He felt drawn to her. His pulse quickened and he felt that same nervous awareness he used to get around pretty girls when he in his awkward teens.

But this was the odd part. Standing before him, highlighted in the darkness by the porch light and his headlights, was a beautiful woman with a sexy figure—the type of woman he used to have wet dreams about—but it wasn't her beauty that drew him in. It wasn't the lure of the naughty pleasure her body could bring him. It wasn't the thrill of her luscious lips tantalizing parts of his body— above and below.

It was the moment of sadness he saw reflected in her hazel-green eyes.

Just before Kahron parked and cut off his truck lights he saw her lips shape into a frown. He opened the driver side door and rose a bit so that she could see him. He liked that her face shifted to surprise and then pleasure— she remembered him as well. In an instant he wanted to be the one to take that sadness from her eyes.

Bianca sat on the top step of the porch waiting for her father's return. She glanced down at her watch. He had been gone for well over seven hours.

"No wonder the business' gone to pot," she muttered, just as headlights reflected in her eyes.

She rose, ready finally to have the conversation with her father that she rehearsed in her head all afternoon.

As the truck neared, she saw that it wasn't her father's vehicle. She looked on as the truck parked next to Trishon's BMW and the drivers door opened.

Her heart swelled as the moonlight glinted off of the top of his silver head. It couldn't be him, could it?

Her eyes locked on him as she looked into his face.

Oh, yes. Yes the hell it was.

Bianca started to walk down the steps to him, but stopped herself. His shades were gone, but it was him and Bianca felt an awareness of him that made her absolutely breathless.

His hair looked so divine against his bronzed complexion that she knew was more sun cooked that heredity.

"Hi. How you doing? Is Hank home?" he asked in a

warm, deep voice that she knew could emit a guttural cry as a woman brought him to a seductive climax.

Breathe, Bianca, breathe.

Then she realized she still hadn't spoke.

Talk, Bianca, talk.

"No, he's not home yet," she said, wanting to do something to stall him from leaving her presence.

"Could you tell him Kahron Strong stopped by?" he asked.

Strong, huh? Like strong loving?

"I'm Bianca. Bianca King," she said suddenly, hating the eagerness of her voice as she went ahead and moved down a step.

It worked to stop him from climbing back into the truck. "Nice to meet you."

"Kahron, huh? That's different?"

"It's a family thing," he said, smiling so broadly that his white teeth gleamed.

Uhm, uhm, uhm.

"That's nothing, my father's name is Kael and my Mom thought it was cute to name us all with a K," he said, actually moving around the open car door to come closer.

A fine sheen of sweat broke out in the valley between Bianca's breasts. Something about this man just did *it* for her.

"So there's Kaleb, Kade, Kaeden, and Kaitlyn."

As Kahron put one booted foot up on the bottom step and leaned casually against the banister, Bianca slowly sank to sit down on the step and looked up at him.

"Wow you have a big family," Bianca said, wrapping her arms around her knees. "I was an only child."

"There are positives and negatives to big families, especially when you add on the uncles, aunts, cousins, nieces, nephews, in-laws, family pets . . ."

At that moment the same lab from earlier today leaned its head over the side of the truck and barked twice as it tongue hung from its mouth like a bell.

Bianca laughed, that inevitable snort escaping her mouth as she did.

Headlights illuminated from the road and Bianca leaned to the left to look, while Kahron looked over his shoulder.

She recognized her father's truck and was filled with relief.

His truck rolled to a stop in front of the house barely missing the rear of Kahron's truck. They both watched as Hank's big body lumbered out of the truck, walking like he had the weight of the world on his broad shoulders.

"Evening, Hank," Kahron greeted, his eyes squinted as he watched the other man.

Hank had been looking down at his feet but his head jerked up at the sound of Kahron's voice. He stopped, wobbling a bit on his feet, as he peered at Kahron as if he saw three of him instead of one. "Oh shit no, Strong. F–f–f–first you . . . you want my land and now . . . and now . . . and now you sniffin' up my daughter's t–t–t–tail. Hell naw I say," Hank ended on a roar, his words slurring together.

Seconds letter he took one lumbering step toward Kahron and swung. When Kahron shifted one step to the right, Hank's body twirled in a full circle before he fell forward to the ground, causing a cloud of dust to rise up around his frame.

Bianca dashed down the stairs to him, immediately surrounded by the acrid fumes of alcohol. She bent, trying to help him to his feet—no easy task.

Kahron stooped to help him as well, but that only sent Hank flying forward again as he jerked away from the younger man.

"Don't t–t–t–t–touch me, Strong," he garbled. "*No* means *no*, you young sh–sh–sh–shit."

Bianca finally helped him to his feet, her arm around his waist, as she guided her father up the stairs. His weight put a strain on her knees as she struggled to hold them both up.

"Good night, Bianca."

She wasn't physically able to turn and look at Kahron—and she regretted that—but she briefly raised her hand to him before entering the house. Soon she heard his truck door slam and the crunch of his tires against the road as he drove away.

"Want my ranch . . . damn vulture," was audible from her father's drunken gibberish. "Bunny . . . home . . . help . . . n–n–n–now . . . there."

Trishon walked into the room as Bianca struggled to get him to a crimson sofa that looked like grotesque, oversized lips. She set a reddish-looking drink on the coffee table and pulled the leopard print throw from the love seat atop him. "Just leave him there. He'll get up after while."

Bianca eyed the drink. "And what is that?"

"A little something to keep him from having a hang-over in the morning," Trishon said over her shoulder, on her way out of the room.

Bianca moved to leave the room as well. She paused at the entrance, her hand on the light switch as she looked back at her father in his drunken stupor.

Nothing at all had changed.

3

Surrounded by the bluest of skies as she lay back naked among a bed of clouds, Bianca smiled mischievously. Kahron knelt at the edge of the clouds between her wantonly open thighs, his lengthy erection in his hand as he massaged the full length of it and then squeezed the thick, smooth tip.

Her eyes devoured every bit of him. From his broad shoulders, to his muscled chest with just the right amount of soft, flat hairs, down to his rigid abdomen. His member was long, thick, and throbbing, just begging to be touched, stroked, and tasted. She found it odd that soft curly hairs surrounding his shaft were ebony—unlike his silver-flecked head.

"Touch it," he demanded huskily, biting his bottom lip.

Her hands moved from above her head to stroke down the length of her silken body. Hotly, her eyes caressed him as she used her slender fingers to open the moist folds of her core. She loved the way his eyes pierced her as she began to pluck the rose colored bud gently, causing the heat to rise in her belly. Bianca purred like a kitten at the pleasure she brought herself, her hips arching to meet her own fingers.

"Oh, Bianca," he moaned throatily, releasing his tool. It rose to slap lightly against his abdomen as he used his hands to grab her strong thighs and jerk her body upwards until her core sat at his chin and her delicate back pressed against his thighs.

"I wonder if it tastes as good as it smells?" he asked, his words blowing softly against her heated and throbbing flesh.

Kahron jerked her body a bit higher until his mouth fit easily over the whole of her wetness and his chin sat smuggled against the delicate crease of her fleshy buttocks. He used his tongue to lick her lips.

Bianca's back arched off his muscled chest as he ate her like he was starved.

The cloud began to slowly spin, rotating about the skies whose hues deepened to violet and crimson. Round and round as he suckled her fleshy bud between his teeth and caused her thighs to quiver.

"Kahron," she gasped. "Yes, yes, yes, yes—"

Brrrnnnggg.

"No," Bianca whimpered as the cloud began to disintegrate from beneath them and she felt her body slipping down the length of Kahron's frame into a blue abyss . . .

Brrrnnnggg.

Bianca sat up in bed, her hands still pressed intimately between her legs, her heart pounding from being abruptly awakened from a dream. A damn good dream.

Disoriented, she looked around the room feeling like she was in purple hell.

Where am I? Holtsville.

What is that noise? Cell phone.

Bianca climbed out of bed, wiping the moisture on

her fingers on her oversized T-shirt before she snatched up the cell phone from where it sat charging on the dresser. "Hello."

"*Bonjour, beau l'un.*"

Bianca rolled her eyes heavenward. "Good morning, Armand," she said, pulling off the satin cap she slept in to protect her curls.

Figures *he* would be the one to wake her from one hell of a wet dream.

"What time is it?" she asked him, her eyes still squinted with sleep as she moved to sit down on the edge of the bed.

"It's noon, *mon cherie.*"

Bianca never slept late. "What can I help you with, Armand?" she asked, ready to get her day rolling.

"*Me permettre de faire l'amour à vous.*"

She released a heavy breath. "No, you cannot make love to me. But you can *se masturber* until your hand falls off," she told him with pleasure.

"Don't tease me," he begged.

Bianca actually laughed.

"Okay, I called because there's an emergency meeting with the United Way and I need a fax number for the admin to send your absentee vote on how to divide the campaign funds this year."

Bianca rose from the bed to walk over to her still packed suitcase. "I'll have to get my Dad's fax number and call you back with it."

"Good. Oh, and Bianca?"

"Goodbye, Armand," she said, hanging up the phone before he could spout another lewd comment in English *or* French.

Bianca didn't even bother calling to check her office, she had a capable staff who didn't need her trying to hover over their work via cell phone. Besides, she wanted to catch up with her Dad before he hauled tail for the day.

She locked her bedroom door and then pulled her nightshirt over her head as she walked into the adjoining bath. It wasn't until she was under the spray of the shower that she thought of her sexy dream about Kahron.

As she lathered her body with her favorite Carol's Daughter body cleansing gel in Jamaican Punch—a heavenly blend of raspberry, peach, jasmine, nutmeg, and cardamon— Bianca wondered if in fact all of the hair on Kahron's body had silvered. Not that it mattered one bit. If he was half as good in real life as he was in her dream, well . . .

The feel of the water pelting against her breasts and the steam rising to press warmly against her skin didn't help the ache of arousal she felt.

It had been so long since a man drew her attention the way Kahron did.

No matter how badly she wanted to feel his long, slender fingers on her nipples, that's not why she was back in town. Especially since she didn't know the reason her father was so angry and rude to the man. Yet another of the gazillion questions she had for her father, and the sooner she got downstairs, the sooner she'd get some answers.

Bianca finished her shower Kahron-free, eventually dressing in fitted jeans and a T-shirt with "SEXY VET" stretched across her ample chest. She didn't bother with make-up, leaving her face smooth and naturally pretty, but she did put on her large diamond hoops and thin chain with a diamond cross pendant—her first gifts to herself once the clinic was out of the red. She wore them always.

Bianca found her father in the dining room nursing a cup of coffee. His eyes were red as fire as he shifted them

away from her. Bianca swallowed all of her reprimands—
for now.

"What happened to the barn?" she asked, crossing her
arms over her chest as she looked down at him.

"Strong burnt it down," Hank growled, his hand
tightly gripping his cup of coffee.

Bianca looked confused. "Are you kidding me? Why
isn't he in jail?" she asked, already reaching in her back
pocket for her cell phone. "I'm calling the police."

Hank shook his head and waved his hand. "No need.
They said there's no sign of arson. Fire department says
faulty wiring."

"What did the insurance company say?"

Hank remained quiet.

"No insurance," Bianca stated, her anger at her father
steadily rising.

Bianca counted to ten as she slid her thin cell phone
back into her pocket. "If this is the case why do you
think Kahron did it?"

"He wants my land," Hanks spouted, slamming his
beefy fist on the dining room table and causing the
coffee in his cup to slosh over the side onto the glass.

Bianca sought patience. "And?"

"I don't trust him. Never did really. Had me fooled
before, but I can see clearly now."

"Because?"

"Around the same time he started making offers to
buy me out somebody's been pulling shenanigans
around my damn ranch."

Now we're getting somewhere.

"Like what, Daddy?"

"Letting the air out my tires, releasing the horses,
contaminating my water supplies, stealing equipment . . .

should I go on?" Hank's ire was evident as he stuck a Marlboro cigarette in his mouth and lit it.

Bianca remained quiet.

"I ain't selling my land!"

"I wish you had the same gusto about not drinking," she drawled.

Hank just glared at her.

Needing a reprieve from his tirade, Bianca just nodded.

"I'm going to take a look at your books today. Is that okay?" she asked, finding it hard to keep the disappointment from her voice.

Hank nodded. "Whatever you want, Bianca."

She crossed the dining room to reach the swinging door leading into the kitchen.

"Bianca, I'm—"

She left the dining room, the *swoosh-swoosh* of the door swinging back and forth ate up his words.

Trishon was at the stove, still dressed in a short and sheer mint green housecoat. She turned to look at Bianca over her shoulder, smiling warmly. "Mornin', Bianca. I'm just finishing breakfast," she said in a cheery voice.

"Good morning," she said. Bianca longed for shades as the screaming orange of the walls caused her eyes to ache. She reached for two tall glasses from the red dish rack and moved over to the adjacent corner to fill one with coffee, creamer, and sugar.

"Your Daddy just loves my scrambled eggs," Trishon said, her southern accent prominent as she lifted the pan to scoop some of the eggs onto a plate.

Bianca carried the glasses to the refrigerator, using the ice maker on the door to fill the empty glass with ice. "Smells good," she said, walking over to the island as she poured the coffee over the ice.

Trishon carried two steaming plates out of the

kitchen, backing out with them in her hand. "Help yourself," she offered.

Bianca sipped her coffee as she peered down into the pan. The eggs looked fluffy enough but there was little reddish-brown flecks in them. Frowning a bit, she used a fork to dig one of the flecks out of the eggs and tasted it. It was a little hard and had a familiar flavor to it . . . kind of like bacon . . . more like—

Bianca eyes widened in recognition and her eyes then noticed the large open container of bacon bits sitting on the counter next to the stove.

"Who puts bacon bits in eggs?" she muttered, deciding right then she wasn't hungry.

Bianca carried her glass out of the kitchen. "Daddy, I'll be in the study. If you'll just meet me in there when you're done with breakfast," she said, continuing toward the hall.

Hank looked like he'd rather eat nails, but he nodded before scooping a pile of eggs into his mouth.

"Actually, Hank has to help me with a quickie—I mean a quick chore upstairs and then he's all yours," Trishon said, reaching over to caress Hank's hand with her index finger as she licked her fork and gazed into his eyes.

Hank's broad face broke into a grin bigger than the state of South Carolina and Bianca had to fight not to frown at the thought of their "chore."

As they shared a kiss over their weird breakfast she gladly left them alone. *Mama must be spinning in her grave.*

He was paid well for what he did, but even he had to wonder to what end did someone want to see the King ranch ruined. Atop a hill in the distance he used binoculars to look down at the King spread. His gaze fell on the convertible Volvo.

King's daughter was back in town. His loins stirred at the thought of her. There was no denying her appeal, but he had not intention of pursuing her. Still, he could dream of those big lips pleasing him.

He laughed at the thought, letting his hand drop to roughly stroke his erection.

She had no idea what she just walked into.

Kahron sat behind his massive black walnut desk in his study, his eyes locked on his phone. He leaned forward in his seat to reach for it but paused, eventually drawing his hand back and leaning back in his chair.

He wanted to call Bianca.

He laughed at his nervousness over simply picking up the phone and calling her.

When he got home last night she had been on his mind: the beauty of her eyes, the sound of her laughter, the subtle scent of her perfume.

But there was more to it than that.

He wanted King's land and although the stubborn drunkard refused, Kahron knew it would be just a matter of time before it was his. So why not sooner than later?

Everyone in town knew Bianca left home for college and never returned. Although Hank bragged on his daughter, the successful veterinarian, it was obvious their relationship had to be strained. Now she was back, and he had to wonder what role did or would Bianca play in all of this?

"Women or money?"

Startled, Kahron looked up to find the oldest of his four brothers, Kade, striding into his study. His square and handsome face filled with surprise and a toothy grin. "Women or money what?" he asked, sitting up in his leather chair.

Kade raked his long fingers through his hair as he folded his tall frame—nearly six foot five—into one of the leather club chairs in front of Kahron's desk. Like all of the Strong men Kade's hair had prematurely grayed in his mid-twenties. He wore his in short, thick curls— a testament to their mother's Native American heritage— that framed his square face. Women liked to say he looked like Rick Fox, N.B.A. player and soon-to-be ex-husband of Vanessa Williams.

"Women or money trouble," Kade answered, leaning forward to place his elbows on his knees in the navy blue Dickies uniform he wore—Kade's preferred gear for working on the family ranch in Walterboro.

Kahron, like Kade and the rest of the Strong boys, considered himself a businessman who owned a ranch, but definitely not a typical cowboy; so, there wasn't a Stetson, tight-fitting Wrangler's jeans, or typical cowboy boots to be found in his wardrobe. They listened to hip-hop, wore Sean John suits for business and Roca-Wear or the like for pleasure. When it came to the necessities of boots for work they all preferred Timberlands or boots of the like.

The Strong men stood out like sore thumbs at the local rodeos and cattle auctions—and that's just the way they liked it.

"Neither," Kahron finally answered, even though an image of Bianca smiling up at him drifted to mind.

"That's what your mouth says," Kade said—an indication that he thought his brother was lying.

"Where's Kadina?" Kahron asked, changing the subject.

"At the ranch. Probably driving Ma crazy as always."

Kahron smiled as he thought of his beautiful six year-old niece. "First grand and she runs the whole family with a smile."

"Bad ass," Kade said with a huge loving grin. "She told me to be home in an hour. Can you believe that?"

"With Kadina? Yes."

"What you getting into tonight?"

Kahron shrugged, thinking he would *love* to get into Bianca King. "Let's call up the Deal twins and ride to Savannah," he offered.

Kade's handsome face immediately closed up. "Naw, I'll pass," he said, throwing his car keys up into the air to catch with ease.

Kahron chose his next words carefully. "It's been a year, Kade," he said almost cautiously, knowing the death of his brother's wife, Reema, was a volatile subject for him.

In just an instant warm hazel eyes froze over. "A year ain't shit, Kahron," Kade answered, his tone cold, yet filled with pain.

"You're right. I'm sorry."

Kade looked up and met his brother's stare with the year's worth of pain he suffered through. "I know you mean well. I even know Daddy throwing every pretty thing between here and Georgia at me is his way of helping, but I'm just not ready."

Kahron felt sadness for his brother weigh his broad shoulders down. If he could swallow down his brother's pain for him, he gladly would. That's how the Strong men were. One for all and all for one.

Last year after his break-up with Shauna, his girl-friend of the last three years, Kahron had to deal with that loss. He took it at his own speed and his family respected that. A break-up was nothing at all like losing someone you love to death. So, if Kade wanted to set his own time to heal, then Kahron respected that.

How could he not? Losing Shauna over foolishness had really gotten to him. He thought he had found "the one," but soon she let small town gossip and lies turn a good relationship into constant battles, lies, and accusations. Never once had Kahron cheated on Shauna, but she wouldn't believe him, so she became like Easy Rawlins, snooping and trying to investigate the truth in his words.

When he discovered that she let her lack of trust lead her to the arms and bed of another man, Kahron walked away from the relationship.

Trust was a major issue with him, particularly in a relationship. Without trust their was no foundation to build upon and at that point anything can happen to jeopardize the love.

"King agree to sell, yet?" Kade asked.

"No, not yet."

"From what I hear it'll be just a matter of time. It's a damn waste, but his lost is your gain."

Kahron his eyes filled with steely determination. "Exactly."

"I'm sorry about last night."

Bianca didn't even bother to look up from the ledger at her father's apology. She had spent the last hour going over his books and right now she wanted explanations more than empty apologies.

Hank rose from the chair, shuffling toward the bar in the corner.

"If you pour a drink I'm out of here. Today. Right now." Bianca eyes went steely. "I mean it."

Hank turned and faced her, pointing his finger at her

in anger. "I'm *your* father, Bianca Renee King, or did you forget that when you ran off."

Bianca met his stare. "No, more like *you* forgot and that's why I left."

Hank turned away from her and settled his hand on the canister. The glass stopper rattled against the glass of the decanter from the trembling in his hands.

Bianca rose from the chair, coming from behind the desk to stand by her father. "This business was failing way before those things started happening three months ago. You're over a hundred thousand dollars in debt, you're behind on your property taxes, you have no income coming in right now, and you have a wife who is spending way too much money."

The rattling increased until the liquid inside the bottle sloshed against the side.

Bianca touched his back. "Things are out of control because you have lost control, Daddy," she told him softly, fighting the tears because now was not the time.

Hank closed his eyes as his grip on the decanter tightened. "You don't understand, Bianca," he told her, his voice tortured.

She released a heavy breath as she licked her suddenly dry lips. "You're right, Daddy, I don't."

His shoulder shook with his tears and Bianca felt like her very soul was on fire. It was never easy to see your parents cry.

"I promise you I will fix this, but I need my Daddy. I need you to be the man you were before Mama died. It's either that liquor or me and this ranch. The choice is yours."

Bianca turned and walked away from him. When she heard him lift the decanter she went weak with sadness and she hugged herself as her tears flowed freely. "Oh, Daddy, why?" she cried, turning to him.

Hank flung the decanter into the barren fireplace with more gusto than she seen in her father in a long time.

Relief flooded her body in waves and she rushed to him, burying her face deep against his chest as his arms surrounded her with bearlike strength.

"This ain't gone be easy, Bunny," he admitted, his chin atop her head.

"I remember a wise man saying that victory never comes easy," she told him, leaning back to smile up at him.

Hank grunted. "A wise man, huh?"

Bianca shrugged. "I'm biased, sue me."

And Hank laughed deep and rich and full in his chest.

"You ready to get to work?" Bianca asked, moving out of his grasp.

Hank released a heavy breath as he moved back to his seat. "Ready as I'll ever be."

"Why do you think Kahron Strong is behind the sabotage?" she asked, as she took the seat behind the desk.

"That bastard," Hank said without missing a beat.

A snapshot of her naughty dream flashed and Bianca literally shook her head to rid it.

"About a month after he came sniffing around asking to buy my land those damn shenanigans started," Hank roared, leaning forward to slam his massive fist down on the desk. "He had the audacity to tell me I could either sell it to him outright or he'd get it one way or another eventually."

Bianca's anger began to stir. Yes, Kahron Strong made her panties moist, but she truly didn't know the man from a can of paint. How badly did he want the King land?

"Did you tell the police?" Bianca asked.

Hank snorted in obvious derision. "Said there's no proof."

"Well, first thing Monday I'm going to pay the property taxes and settle some of these bills," Bianca said, hating the disappointment she felt that Kahron Strong might very well be her enemy.

"Bunny, you can't—"

Bianca nodded as she tallied the bills on a calculator. "I can and I will."

"Bunny—"

Bianca held up her hand as she pierced him with her eyes. "Daddy, trust me, right now you got bigger fish to fry then worrying about how I spend my money."

Hank look at her with curiosity. "The booze, huh?"

Bianca nodded. "Oh definitely that *and* you have to tell Trishon there's a freeze on all outgoing funds effective immediately."

Hank's face fell and he looked like telling his wife that bit of news was far harder then giving up the liquor.

Trishon parked her vehicle outside the Belks department store in Walterboro. She went sashaying into one of the few stores in the small town where you could buy designer clothing.

She really wasn't looking for anything in particular. She just needed to get out of the house. With Hank and his precious Bianca holed up in his study, she felt a little . . . left out.

She would never admit it to a living soul, but Bianca intimidated her with her smarts and her money. Trishon hadn't met too many women that made her doubt herself, especially since the day she snagged Hank King. Once she became Mrs. King she finally got the respect she always felt she deserved. Money had a way of getting respect in a small southern town.

When people saw her they saw a wealthy man's wife, not the picky head little girl who grew up in a 14 × 60 metal trailer that didn't have running water or nearly enough space to accommodate the six children who lived their with their mother, grandmother, and aunt—all of whom were considered "slow" by the townspeople and the state.

Many a night they had nothing but dreams of food for dinner. When they did have food it was hardly a feast with stuff like fried salt pork and dry rice. Once they ate just the pot liquor that was left from collard greens they had the week before.

She always knew she wanted—and was going to have—better.

The only thing Trishon thought she had going for her was the way men liked to be in her company and tell her she was pretty and buy her nice things. So, she learned from a young age how to get what she wanted with what she had.

Most times she hated the feel of the men's hands and the sounds of their grunting as they pumped away between her cold thighs, but sometimes—every once in a while—a man's hands would warm her, soothe her, and make her feel wanted for the first time in a long time.

It didn't matter if they didn't have the decency to buy a nice hotel room to fill her with their desire. They would park deep in the woods in their cars and whisper heated words of her beauty in the back seat. Only to ignore her in the light of day.

But that was behind her now.

"How are you today, Mrs. King?"

Trishon looked up surprised by the saleswoman's voice behind her. She smiled, pushing away her memories. "I'm fine, just fine," she said.

Yes, she was Mrs. Hank King, and the days of hunger, shame, poverty, and pity were long behind her.

4

Sunday afternoon after fighting her way though Trishon's dinner of meatloaf with a cornflake crust and mash potatoes—with the skin—Bianca turned her Volvo down the drive leading to Circle S Ranch. Finding the ranch hadn't been a problem because Kahron had purchased the old MacDonald Farm and Bianca had spent many a lazy afternoon playing on the ranch with her then-childhood friend Sara.

It was obvious to see the improvements Kahron made, having grown up on a ranch and working on ranches as a vet. Bianca had to admit she was impressed.

But she wasn't there to survey the land.

Bianca pulled in front of the house. Kahron was leaning against the back of a pick-up truck talking to a tall, slender guy with a short 'fro. They both looked up as she slowed her vehicle.

Kahron's eyes were shaded by his ever-present aviator shades, but Bianca knew he was looking at her. Her pulse raced as she came to a stop beside them.

"Are you behind the sabotage of my father's business?" she asked, cutting to the chase.

Kahron stared at her for a long time and she wondered what he was thinking.

"I didn't know there was any sabotage going on," he told her, turning his head back to the ranch hand he was talking with. "Excuse me for a sec, Dante."

"Sure thing, boss."

Kahron walked toward her car. "How are you today, Bianca?" he asked in a calm manner as he placed his hands on the door and leaned down a bit to stare at her.

Bianca felt overwhelmed by his presence, but she had to remind herself that this man might be trying to ruin her father's business—what little business there was left. Visions of riding him naked and wild astride a horse just weren't appropriate—no matter how enticing.

"I'd be doing a whole lot better if you'd leave my father the hell alone," she told him, forcing a coldness to her tone that she honestly didn't feel.

Kahron's jaw tightened and although she couldn't see those eyes, she could easily imagine them filled with irritation or even anger.

He opened her car door and then stepped back to wave his hand toward the house in some misguided attempt at an invitation to take the conversation inside.

Bianca looked up him, indignant at his forwardness. She leaned over in her seat to close the door back. "When you take over paying the car note then you can run this," she told him with spunk, just before it slammed close.

"Why all this anger? Where's the lady I was talking to last night? What's your problem, beside the fact that your obviously bull-headed like your daddy," Kahron told her.

Bianca let the bull-headed comment slide . . . for now. "My problem is someone trying to ruin my father, that's what," she told him.

"So I guess I forced your father to drink his life away," he bit out.

The truth cut like a knife, but Bianca blinked away any show that his words hit home. Instead she flung the car door open.

"Umph."

The door had hit against Kahron's legs and Bianca got pleasure from that.

Kahron frowned deeply.

Take that. Bianca faced him and then waved her hand toward the stairs leading into *his* house. "Whenever you're ready," she said, as he continued to stare at her through those shades she wanted to snatch off his face and stomp on.

Kahron used his knee to nudge the car door until it swung close, before he led the way up the stairs. When he got to the door he stepped aside. "My office is the first door on the right," he said in a low and intimate voice near her ear as she breezed past him to enter the foyer. "Be back in a sec, Dante."

"Okay, boss."

Bianca shook off the shiver of awareness he caused. Her eyes quickly took in as much of his home as she could as she walked to his office. Everything was in warm, masculine tones with clean lines and for some reason that surprised her.

It was then—for the first time—that she wondered if he was married. Was there a Mrs. Kahron to stroke her fingers across that hellified body?

Good time to ask, Bianca thought as she recalled her dream.

"My father's business isn't for sale," Bianca said as she entered the room. "No matter what."

She turned to face him as he strode in behind her, but

her eyes and lips rounded in surprise when he pushed his shades atop his head and didn't stop moving forward until he was standing in front her and clasping her face with his calloused hands.

Thump-thump.

That was the double-beat of her heart.

Bianca stepped back and Kahron stepped forward, his hands still there on her cheeks—warm and enticing.

Thump-thump-thump-thump.

"What are you doing?" she asked, as she tried to step back from him.

"What I wanted to do since I first laid eyes on you, B," Kahron whispered softly, the pressure of his cool breath against her lips increasing as his head lowered to hers.

She gasped and her mouth filled with his breath just as his lips pressed down upon hers. *Jesus*, she thought, before a sweet moan of nothing but pure pleasure escaped from the back of her throat.

Thump–thump–thump–thump–thump . . .

Kahron lightened the pressure of his hands when he felt no resistance, but he deepened the kiss, lightly tracing her full, plump lips before his tongue eased inside to circle her own.

Thump–thump–thump–thump–thump–thump–thump–thump–thump–thump . . .

Bianca shifted her head from the right to the left as Kahron began to lightly suckle the tip of her tongue. *Oh, see that . . . now that feels good.* She lifted her hands to lightly grasp his sides, vaguely taking in the hard ripples of his abdomen beneath her clinging fingers.

She became aware of a movement down her abdomen, stopping at the top of her thigh. Pressure. Hardness. Length. Thickness. Trouble. Bianca's eyes widened in shock and . . . well, fascination. *Oh My God, is all that his . . .*

Thump–thump–thump–thump–thump–thump–thump–thump–thump–thump–thump–thump–thump–thump–thump–thump–thump–thump–thump . . .

Bianca used her teeth to clamp down lightly on that wily tongue of his, even as the bud between her legs throbbed with a beat all its own.

Kahron's eyes opened as he stared down at her in surprise.

Their eyes locked.

Hers were defiant.

His amused.

She released him and stepped away from him. "I'd advise you to keep it to yourself in the future," she warned him, crossing her arms over her chest to help put pressure on her aching and taut nipples.

"Now why would I do that when you seemed to be enjoying it so much?" he teased, moving to sit at his desk.

"Woulda been better if you had a Tic-Tac," she lied.

Kahron just threw his head back and laughed.

She stared at him with her finely arched brow raised. In truth she was more angry at herself than him. Her intention was to give him a piece of her mind . . . not her tail!

"Why do you want my father's ranch so bad?" she asked.

"I want the land," he answered simply.

"How far will you go to get it?" she returned, as she stepped closer to his desk and stared down at him. "There's a burnt barn I'm curious about," she said, even though she wasn't one hundred percent sure the barn had been vandalized.

Kahron tilted his head up to look at her. "The authorities

say it was an accident. Word on the street is your father probably did it for the insurance."

She didn't bother to tell him her father didn't even have property insurance on the barn.

"What you fail to understand—no matter how many times I tell you—your father doesn't need help ruining his business," he said, rising from his chair.

Bianca eyes darted to his lips and she hated herself for it. "Since you know so much about the 'word on the street,' make sure you get the word out that King Equine Service isn't for sale. If I find out who the a-hole is with the spare time on his hands to harass my father, I'll make sure they'll regret it, and that includes you, Kahron," she told him in steely tones she was proud of, before turning to leave him and the odd chemistry they made in the room.

"Bianca," he called out to her.

Moments later a warm hand circled her forearm.

Bianca whirled around, her face confused.

Kahron let his hand rise to lightly hold her chin. "I promise you I haven't done anything to sabotage your father's business," he told her huskily, his eyes measuring hers.

Bianca's eyes searched his.

"Let me take you to dinner?" he asked in that sexy and raspy voice of his.

Acute awareness shimmied over Bianca and she wondered what drew her to this man. She tilted her head back to free his hand from her chin. "I don't think so," she answered, turning and walking out the house.

Kahron stood to one of the windows lining the front wall of his office. He watched as Bianca walked to her car. She paused, turned, and started back toward the house. His heart stopped. She turned again, walked back to her car and got in, eventually driving off. He stood there until she turned the car down the long dirt road leading to the main highway.

Bianca spent the rest of the day trying to come up with a plan to save the ranch. It was about more than money. She could just float the cash into the business to keep it going, but if her father's reputation was destroyed and people didn't trust him to get the job done, then the money was useless.

She rose from where she sat on the top step of the porch to lean against the rail. She crossed her arms over her chest as she listened to the sounds of a sweet summer Carolina night.

There was so much that needed to be done and certainly more than she could do in two weeks—and that included making sure her father got sober.

How she could expect his old clients to have renewed faith in him when she had none?

"Oh, Daddy," she said with a heavy release of breath.

Throwing the bottle of liquor in the fireplace had been a grand and dramatic gesture, but it didn't really guarantee that he would never drink again.

Her father's sobriety. Repairing the barn. Ordering inventory. Recruiting new business. Trying to woo back old business. Hiring staff. Trishon's spending. And, oh Lord, Trishon's cooking.

One was bad enough, but all of them combined was going to send her to Charter, the mental hospital in Columbia.

And that's *if* her growing infatuation with Kahron Strong didn't jack her up first.

"Whoo," Bianca sighed, her eyes slowly closing as she remembered the taste of the man. His scent. His touch. His hardness.

Impressive hardly seemed the right word to describe it.

I promise you I haven't done anything to sabotage your father's business.

Bianca was usually a good judge of character and her first impression of Kahron had not made her think he was untrustworthy, deceptive, or criminal-minded. Her father thought he was behind the fire *and* the man admitted he wanted the land, but then, how reliable was her father's opinion?

Had the fire department been wrong in their assessment of the fire's cause? What of the other pranks? They seemed mild in comparison to burning a barn.

It just made sense that Kahron would be the one to benefit most from Hank being in a situation where he had to sell his business.

I promise you I haven't done anything to sabotage your father's business.

"Oh, hi Bianca. I didn't know you were out here."

She turned to find Trishon stepping out onto the porch, a pack of cigarettes and a lighter in her hand. Bianca hated smoking and certainly didn't want to intake second-hand smoke, but she remained quiet. "Just getting some air."

Trishon just nodded and moved to lean forward against the railing as she exhaled a long and thin line of silver smoke.

"Do you know Kahron Strong very well?" Bianca asked, curious about the man.

Trishon tilted her head a little to look at Bianca as she

placed the cigarette back between her lips. "Well enough I guess. Why?"

Bianca shrugged, turning her head back to look ahead at the shadow of the treetops against the night sky. "Daddy thinks he's behind the fire," she said.

"From what I hear he wants the land bad enough."

"Yes, but the authorities said it was the wiring," Bianca insisted, not sure if she was trying convince Trishon or herself.

"Like they can't be wrong."

"Outside of that, though, you ever heard anything bad about him?" Bianca asked.

"Aw hell, he ain't no saint, Bianca," Trishon spouted, flicking her cigarette to send the ashes circling into the night air.

Bianca leveled her eyes on the woman and fell silent.

"He's a heartbreaker, too. That's one dog I'd stay clear of if I was you," Trishon added, as she raised her hand to cover the next cigarette she was lighting.

"I can lookout for myself, but thanks."

Another stream of smoke. "Poor Shauna cries behind his cheatin' ass *all* the time."

Bianca felt her stomach drop—if that was at all possible. *Who in the hell was Shauna?*

"That's his girlfriend," Trishon answered, as if reading Bianca's thoughts.

"That man's personal business is of no concern to me," Bianca added, even though she felt oddly betrayed by the news.

It was Trishon's turn to fall silent.

"Daddy sleeping?"

Trishon tilted her head back to blow smoke rings through her pursed scarlet lips. "He's watching one of them cowboy movies he loves so much."

Bianca smiled softly. "He loves John Wayne, of all things."

The women fell silent again and nothing but the sound of night creatures filled the air.

"I love your father, Bianca."

Bianca bit her bottom lip, her eyes narrowing as she stared off in the distance. "That's good to know," was all she said.

"And he loves me."

Bianca felt the woman's eyes on her so she fought not to roll her own eyes heavenward. "Trishon—"

"I know the reason you haven't been home all these years is 'cause of me," she said, dropping the cigarette to flatten beneath her shoe.

"That's a piece of it, yes," Bianca admitted, turning to face her.

"I know what people say about me in this town, but it was hard growing up the way I did." Trishon's eyes filled with angry tears. "And I made a lot of mistakes, but that's in the past. Don't hold my past against me, Bianca King."

Bianca knew what she said was true. Everyone in town knew the story of Ruby Haddock and her kids. It was no secret how they struggled to survive. How horribly they used to be either teased in their faces or talked about behind their backs.

Yes, she could see how a woman like Trishon had been looking for love in all the wrong places.

"We don't have to be friends, but don't judge me," Trishon said, turning to walk back in the house.

Didn't she have enough drama on her plate?

Needing a diversion, Bianca bent to scoop her cell phone up from the porch. Quickly she dialed.

The line rang for what seemed a million times.

"Whoever this is you owe me a *stiff* one, sugar. And that's a drink if you're a lady and a lay from the fellas."

Bianca smiled at the sound of Mimi's nasal voice. "How's Atlanta, Ms. Mimi?"

"Hey, honey. How's Hootersville?" Mimi squealed.

"That's Holtsville."

"Yeah . . . sure, Sweetie, like it really matters."

You had to know Mimi—really know her—not be offended.

"How's my house?" Bianca asked.

"Smaller than mine, sugar." Mimi laughed like *that* was the funniest thing she ever heard. "I'm kidding. I'm kidding. Its fine."

"Good."

"Hey, you, what's wrong? You sound like a fag who lost his bag of balls."

"Just a lot to do down here. My father needs me—"

"And you love that he needs you, don't you, Sweetie?" Mimi asked softly in a rare show of sympathy and concern.

"Better late than never."

Suddenly the hairs on the nape of Bianca's nape stood on end. She whirled, thinking someone had stepped out onto the porch with her. Nothing. She whirled to look at the sides of the house. The yard was empty. Not a sole to be seen.

But Bianca felt like she was being watched.

Slowly, she looked around at her surroundings again, her body stiff—as if that made her hearing better.

"Bianca, you there? If I wanted to listen to dead silence I would stayed married to Arnold, Sweetie."

Calm down, Bianca, she admonished herself, relaxing her stance.

"I'm here, just felt creepy all of a sudden. Just . . . I don't know, like somebody's watching me."

"Now I know you're stressed, you're quoting Rapwell, darling."

Bianca actually smiled. "Don't you mean, Rockwell?"

"Yeah, whoever."

When she turned suddenly to look around her, he stepped back under the cloak of the bushes. His heart raced as he licked the growing perspiration from his upper lip.

He stood in the bushes and watched her as she talked on her cell phone. Under the light from the porch he saw the uneasiness disappear from her face.

Suddenly she flung her head back and laughed.

His eyes narrowed.

He knew he should leave, but he stood there and watched her until she walked into the house.

Trishon slipped her nude frame between the sheets beside her husband. Reaching across him, her plush breasts pressed into his side as she picked up the remote and turned off the television.

"Huh, what . . . I'm not sleeping," Hank said, lifting his head from his pillow as he wiped the back of his large hand across his mouth.

"Ssshhh."

"I been meaning to talk you," he began. "I need you to cut back on your spending until I get my business back on its feet."

Under the cloak of darkness, she cuddled close to his side. "Oh, Teddy Bear, I don't spend that much, do I?" she asked.

"Right now its more than I have to spend."

"Are these your words or your daughter's?" she asked gingerly.

"Don't bring Bianca into this," he returned sternly, his hand stopping her from caressing his stirring arousal.

Trishon backed off the subject . . . for now.

5

"How in the hell am I supposed to get everything done in two weeks?" Bianca asked herself as she put her chin in her hand and looked out the window of the study. She ignored the accordion folder of her father's important papers she had been reviewing.

Her plans to shoot down to Holtsville and save the day were getting waylaid by reality. The cost of this adventure was building if Bianca carried through with her plans to revitalize the business—plans that included the same PR blitz and business savvy she used to make her clinic the success it was. They discussed replacing the destroyed barn with a prefab metal barn, but the cost was nothing to play with. That plus the cost of restocking the ranch—all without knowing if their clients would return—was a hell of a gamble.

Bianca did think it could be done. It was all a matter of rebuilding faith.

Bianca massaged her own neck as she thought of her clinic. She missed the horses and other animals she loved so much most of all, but rebuilding King Equine

Service presented something to her that the clinic hadn't been for a long time . . . a challenge.

She could extend her stay until her father and the ranch were back on their feet, and maybe travel home on the weekends. But how much time could she afford to take away from her own life and business back in Atlanta? Decisions had to be made and soon because Bianca refused to see the family business ruined.

She needed a diversion so she moved to the small radio in the corner and sped through the channels until she found a hip-hop station, Z93 Jamz. As Keyshia Cole's "I Should Have Cheated" played Bianca danced to the center of the study and starting singing along with the music in her biggest voice.

Bianca was just taking it back to the old school with the cabbage patch dance when she turned and saw Kahron leaning in the doorway watching her. She froze mid–cabbage patch.

He smiled and dropped his head as he uncrossed his arms and pushed off the doorframe to walk into the room. "Don't let me interrupt you," he told her.

Bianca cleared her throat and patted her straw set curls as she moved over to the radio to turn Keyshia off. "Don't you knock?" she asked as she moved over to reclaim her seat behind the desk, shoved the papers back into the accordion folder, and put the folder in the bottom desk drawer.

"I did, you were busy, and I saw you were in here through the window, so . . ."

Bianca eyes took him—drew him in—and she had no complaints. The white T-shirt he wore was snug and fit against his chest, so beautifully offset by the bronze of his skin. His jeans hung lower than ever on his narrow hips below a big rodeo-style belt buckle. "What can I help you with?"

He smiled. Slow and cocky, devilish and confident.

Bianca had to bite her inner cheek to keep from returning the rogue's grin. She gave him a nonchalant look instead.

"Actually, I wanted to talk you and your father, if he's around," Kahron said, stepping forward.

"So, this is business—"

"Oh we can *make* it pleasure," he interrupted easily as his eyes dipped to her lips.

"What would Shauna say?" Bianca asked, wishing as soon as she said the words that she could inhale them back.

Kahron moved to prop himself on the edge of the desk as he looked down at Bianca. "I don't know what she would say, but I'm sure whatever it is she would say it to her boyfriend."

Bianca felt the heat radiate from his body like a warm touch, teasing her nipples into tautness and lightly stroking the bud between her legs until it throbbed with a pulse all its own. She crossed her legs. "Either way its none of my business, Kahron."

"It could be," he returned huskily.

Bianca's chest felt light as air at that.

"No."

Kahron nodded as he reached down to pick up her hand. "Yes."

"*No*," Bianca stressed, pulling her hand away from his heated grasp as she leaned back in the chair.

Kahron rose and moved around the desk.

Bianca swallowed hard and pushed back with her feet until the chair hit the wall with a solid *thump*.

He bent over and placed one hand on each of the arm rests of the chair.

Bianca, this man may be trying to ruin your father. He can't be trusted.

Deep down, however, Bianca didn't believe it.

"Can I kiss you again?" he asked low in his throat as he lowered his handsome square face just inches above hers.

Bianca slowly moved her head from side to side.

He lowered his head anyway until the subtle in and out of his breathing softly whispered against her lips. Her nose nearly touched his and she could see how long and full each individual eyelash was. And his lips. They were lips made to kiss and be kissed . . . by her.

Just one taste.

It was Bianca that closed the minute distance between their lips with a simple raising of her chin. His eyes closed and those lashes fanned against his strong cheekbones as he deepened the kiss from her simple peck to his passionate torture.

They both moaned at the feel of their tongues gently circling one another as their lips pressed together. When Kahron lightly bit her bottom lip before sucking it gently, Bianca felt she could—and would—come right then.

"Bianca!"

Her eyes widened at the sound of her father yelling her name. *Damn, is he psychic?* She twisted to the left to free her lips, toppling out of the chair. She had just scrambled to her feet and moved to stand by the radio when her father's bearlike presence filled the doorway of the study.

Kahron just rose slowly.

"What is *he* doing here?" Hank snapped, his eyes narrowing as he leveled them on Kahron.

Uh-oh. Bianca was not in the mood to referee. "Have a seat, Daddy," Bianca said in a tone that made it seem the most simple request in the world. She looked at Kahron as she waved her hand toward one of the chairs in front of the desk and she took the other.

Maybe if she stayed calm her father would as well. Bianca literally crossed her fingers.

Kahron moved to take the seat next to Bianca.

"I don't know what this about, but I don't like it one damn bit," Hank bit out, even though he did as Bianca bid and moved to take the seat behind the desk. It didn't stop him from glaring at Kahron like he was a pile of manure on his new boots.

"Okay, Mr. Strong, you wanted to talk to us," Bianca began, as if she hadn't just suckled the faint taste of bubble gum from his lips and tongue.

Kahron looked at her with a lazy smile before he turned his head to look Hank King in the eye—man to man. "First, I want to clear the air about your belief that I've been trying to ruin your business," Kahron began.

Hank banged his fist on top of the desk, before he pointed a beefy finger at Kahron as he leaned forward in the chair. "Liar," he roared.

"No, I'm not a liar, and you know that Hank," Kahron returned calmly. "Before I made the offer to buy the ranch you and I got along well. And you know I'm a man of my word. I value my integrity. I've always dealt with every man fairly."

Bianca's eyes flittered about his face looking for a hint of deception.

"Greed has made many a man dirty in his deeds." Hank reached into his shirt pocket and removed a pack of cigarettes.

"There's nothing else I can say to make you believe me," Kahron said. "But my offer to buy still stands."

Bianca's doubts returned. The man was determined to get his hands on the land. She wondered if he was determined enough to trifle with her feelings for it.

"Well it ain't for sale you little hard-headed shit," Hank said, his cigarette hanging precariously from his bottom lip.

"I know King Equine Services looks pretty washed up to you right now, but my father and I have every intention of revitalizing this business," Bianca began, her voice firm as she met his stare. "Now, your unwillingness to accept the fact that this is a new era for this business . . . your determination in purchasing this land although you have been told on many occasions that it isn't for sale . . . makes me wonder to what end are you willing to go to make it for sale."

"Exactly," Hank chimed in.

"Bianca, you don't believe that," Kahron said in a voice that seemed sad or disappointed.

"Then let it go," she stressed to him softly as she met his gaze.

Kahron stood. "I won't make the offer again, but I will be honest. If the opportunity arises I will own this ranch."

Bianca was surprised by the pang of hurt she felt. "Thanks for the faith," she said bitterly.

"It's not you that I don't have the faith in, Bianca."

"Get out, Strong," Hank roared, rising to his feet so forcefully that the chair rolled back and slammed against the wall.

Kahron looked at Bianca one last time before he walked out the study.

"Can you believe his nerve?"

Bianca crossed her legs. "Before he wanted to buy the ranch would you say he was a honest man?" she asked.

"Wolf in sheep's clothing."

Bianca rose and picked up the notepad with the things she needed to order from her father's supplier. "You better look over this list and see if I left anything out," she said, forcing normalcy to her voice.

Hank reached into the top drawer of the desk and removed his reading glasses. "We don't need a new pressure washer. Papa Doc has mine and I can just get it back from him." Hank said before using a pencil to cross it off the list.

"How's he doing?" Bianca asked of her father's childhood best friend, glad for the diversion.

"Same-o–same-o," Hank said, as he continued to scroll down the list.

"Did you talk to Trishon?" she asked, as she tilted her head to look down at the changes he was making on the list.

"Uh-huh."

Bianca nodded and she took a little breath before she asked her next question. "And how are you doing?"

Hank looked up at her in confusion. "I'm fit as fiddle, Bunny."

"That's not what I mean," she told him in total seriousness.

Hank looked back down at the list. "One day at a time, baby girl. So far so good."

Kahron grimaced as he lowered his nude muscular frame beneath the steaming depths of the water in his oversized claw-foot tub. With a deep moan of contentment he slid down beneath the water until his head rested back against the rim.

He heard Hershey's nail click-click against the floor and looked over at the door just as she nudged it open with her head and entered. She came to sit beside the tub. "Hey, girl. You missed me today?" he asked.

She snorted.

After he returned from the King's he rode Midnight out to the south range, where the men were repairing the water pipes. Long, hard, but very satisfying work.

His body deserved this treat.

It also deserved a good hot meal, and because he had yet to find any new prospects for a housekeeper he would have to throw something together for himself. Just like he washed his clothes and cleaned his own house.

He didn't mind the house chores, but after a long day working the ranch he wanted just to come home and sleep in preparation for the next long day. His father told him he needed a wife, but Kahron was reluctant. He respected the institution of marriage far too much to grab the first eligible bachelorette willing to be his maid.

Suddenly, a vision of Bianca smiling up at him teased him in the steam rising from the tub. She was sexy as all get out, not classically beautiful like Halle Berry or Vivica Fox, but intriguing and beguiling nonetheless.

And she had the most incredible lips. Kissing them was like pressing your lips to the softest clouds. Amazing how the feel of something so soft could make a man so hard: lips, breasts, thighs, and buttocks.

He found himself thinking of Bianca quite a bit, but in truth he really knew nothing about her. The fact that he always let his hormones overrule his head might be the reason for that. When he was in her presence he had to learn to cool his heels—along with other parts of the anatomy—so he might have an actual conversation with the woman and not just give in to the desire to kiss her.

He smiled at the memory of Bianca actually kissing him first today. Lord, that woman knew how to work her tongue.

He felt a cool breeze against the juicy tip of his penis and cocked open one eye to see it standing up erect from between his strong thighs. "Down boy," he said, even as his hands moved to massage the full, thick length of it.

He wanted to know Bianca. He wanted to see more of that side of her where she let loose and just had fun— like when he caught her dancing all alone today.

He also wanted to bury his shaft so deeply inside of her that he felt lost. This was the side of him that seemed to win out whenever he was in her presence.

Maybe, just maybe, if he learned to close the door on that side of his brain—and his penis—that belonged to the horny adolescent in him, he might actually get to know her better. Something he honestly wanted to do.

There was so many things he wanted to know about.

Was she really a big time horse vet back in Atlanta? Was she dating anyone back home—he couldn't believe at least a few hard heads weren't sniffing around her skirts. Why did it take her so long to return home? How long was she staying in town?

Word on the street—which was like the gospel to small town southern folk—was just two weeks.

In terms of him romancing her that was a downer. If he succeeded in getting her to spend time with him, what would they do when she returned home?

In terms of him getting his hands on that ranch, it was a plus. Kahron had no doubts that Bianca could completely get the business back up and running, but as soon as Hank King was back in charge, the man would surely run it in the ground again. At the first hint of delinquent taxes and the land going up for auction by the county, Kahron had every intention of being the one to outbid anyone else for ownership.

Kahron relaxed his body in the water hoping the tightness in his groin would ease, but whenever he cocked open a eye to check, the thick tip of his erection poked through the water to wink back at him. He tried to think neutral thoughts, but everything led back to Bianca.

The remaining water lines they had to lay tomorrow made him think of Bianca naked and wanton as she worked the pipes.

He focused on the rodeo coming to town next month, but that turned to Bianca—gloriously naked in nothing but a Stetson and boots as she rode a bronco.

Kahron tried to ponder what he would fix for himself for dinner. No luck again. Images of Bianca spread eagle atop the island in the center of his kitchen made his thighs quiver and his shaft harden further.

He used his foot to push up the knob for the cold water. As the cold water began to dominate the heat, it was only then that he was able to relax as his erection eased and he found relief.

Shaking his head, he lowered himself until his silver head was submerged beneath the water.

Bianca eyes bore into her father until he was all she saw. Trishon and their dinner guest, Papa Doc, faded into nothing. The dining room darkened to black. She saw or heard nothing but her father.

And he was drunk.

"Pa–pa–pa–pa–pa . . . damn, you crazy, man."

His stuttering was evidence of that. He only stuttered when he was drinking.

She had long since stopped pretending to eat Trishon's dinner of spaghetti made with chunks of spam. Bianca would stare at him until he met her eyes—something he hadn't done since she first bore her eyes into him.

"Bianca, it's good to see you," Papa Doc said in that loud and booming voice of his. He and Hank were similar in build and when they were younger people thought them to be brothers. They were the best of friends and both knew they could rely on each other. "I remember when you were a little girl, running behind your Daddy and me. Daddy's little girl."

"I'm all grown now, Papa Doc," Bianca said, her eyes still locked on her father.

The room went quiet.

Hank looked over at Bianca and then quickly looked back down at his plate as he folded his arms on the table. "You'll always be my little girl," he said.

Bianca said nothing. She got what she wanted for tonight. She wanted him to look her in the face when he knew she was fully aware that he was drinking. He did that. She just rose from her chair and walked from the room.

Her steps carried her right out of the house and down the steps to her car.

Bianca had no idea where she was going. All she knew was that she wanted away from her father and that house. She turned the key in the ignition and the motor purred to life.

What more did she have to do to make him be the father that she once knew and loved to distraction?

How much more money did she have to spend?

How much time away from her life in Atlanta would she have to give up?

How long would she have to pretend that it didn't piss her off how he sat back and let Trishon turn their home into some tribute to gaudiness?

How long would he choose liquor over her?

Why had his love for her faded when her mother died?

Bianca didn't even realize she was crying until she tasted the saltiness of her tears.

She didn't realize that she was headed straight to Kahron, until she parked in front of his house.

Without giving herself a chance to think twice, she turned off the car and raced up the stairs. She used the tail of her t-shirt to wipe the tears from her face before she knocked on the door.

For what seemed long moments, Bianca stood there.

Suddenly a cool draft kissed her face as the door swung open.

6

Kahron stood there, looking down at Bianca in surprise, as he held together the edges of the chocolate towel draped loosely around his waist with one strong grasp. "Bianca, hey, uhm, yeah, hey, come on in," he said, seeming a little put off.

Bianca eyes darted down to his towel and her cheeks reddened. "Wow," she said huskily, lowly, like in reverence.

She didn't think. She just reacted. She followed an instinct. A desire. A want.

Bianca jumped up onto Kahron, wrapping her legs and arms around him as she pressed her lips to his with a wild moan that was a tad bit savage in nature.

Kahron's eyes widened as he stumbled backwards, nearly losing his footing as his arms flayed out comically. He held them out to his side to gather his balance as Bianca began to suckle his lips like she was thirsty.

He reached out with one masculine hand to make the door swing close solidly. When he felt the draft against his privates Kahron realized his towel was no longer around him.

He felt his nature rise and lengthen in one swift action as Bianca sought and found a spot behind his ear to stroke with her tongue.

"Bianca. Bianca. B–b–b–b– . . . damn," he swore, enjoying himself, but definitely conflicted.

Something just didn't feel right. It was all *too* freaky—a first for him. She was wild and anxious, sucking deeply on his neck.

"Ow," he howled out as she nipped too deeply. "Alright, baby, take it easy."

With his arm securely around her waist he bent over to scoop up his towel and then walked into his living room with Bianca still writhing wildly against his body in a decidedly distracting fashion.

She purred as she again moved to capture his lips with her own. "Come on, Kahron. This is what you want. You know it is."

"Oh hell yeah," he said, without thinking.

Bianca unwrapped her legs and slid down his body, smiling as her legs tightened around each side of his erection hanging awkwardly from his body like a thick limb. She stepped back to tear her T-shirt over her head to fling away.

Kahron's mouth shaped into an O as he grimaced in pure appreciation of the sight she made in her lacy brassiere. He hurried to cover himself with the towel. It tented around his hardened penis. He held out his hand to her as she stepped toward him. "No," he shouted.

Bianca jumped on him again and they went flying backwards onto the couch.

* * *

Bianca looked down into Kahron's handsome face and she saw his confusion. "Don't you want me?" she asked, hating the emotions that began to build in her chest.

Anger. Frustration. Pain.

Her eyes filled with tears.

Sadness. Disappointment. Frustration.

The tears fell.

Kahron's face filled with concern. "Hey, hey, what's wrong?" he asked as he used his thumbs to wipe the tears.

"Can we just do this?" she asked in a resigned tone, as she sniffled.

"Not like this. No," he immediately countered.

Bianca rose from his lap to walk over and retrieve her T-shirt from where it hang on the lampshade. She pulled it over her head slowly, as if drained of energy.

Kahron secured the towel around his waist as he moved over to her and turned her to gather her into his arms. He pressed her face against the smoothness of his chest as he lightly sat his chin atop her head.

Bianca inhaled the scent of masculine soap and enjoyed the comfort of his arms. It felt so good to be held, or rather held up.

And in the shelter of his arms—this man who was really no more than a stranger to her—she gave in to all the long buried emotions, and she cried that kind of gut wrenching cry like a child, her body wracked with the tears. She wrapped her arms around his waist and held onto him for dear life.

Kahron rocked her gently as she gave in to the sadness he saw in her eyes from the very beginning. There were stories behind the tears. Stories he wanted to hear. Stories he wanted to help her forget.

As she squeezed a bit closer and buried her face deeper against his chest, his body began to betray him. As his loins stirred to life again, Kahron pulled his lower half away from hers, hoping she wouldn't feel his erection.

It was so childish, but Bianca made him feel that way.

He could have easily made love to her tonight, but he wanted more from her than that. Standing here holding her as she felt safe enough to give in to her emotions made him feel more alive and more wanted than someone looking to him as a sexual conquest.

Even as her tears began to subside, he didn't want to release her. He liked the feel of this woman in his arms. In his life. In his home.

Bianca tilted her head and looked up at him with a soft smile on her splendid lips and mouthed, "thank you."

His heart flipped and he knew he was in trouble.

Bianca stepped back out of Kahron's arms. "I'm sorry I went a little crazy," she told him as she crossed her arms over her chest.

"It's okay," he told her. "You wanna talk about it?"

Bianca shrugged a little. "Yes . . . no . . . I don't know. It's so many things I've just kept inside for a long time, you know. I guess it all just bubbled to the surface tonight."

Kahron nodded as he stood there with his hands on his hips and that devilish towel gaped open at the thigh. "I'm here to listen whenever you're ready."

Bianca looked at him—really looked at him—and her mouth gaped open a bit as she felt her throat go dry.

His chest was broad and square with a fine sprinkle of hair that narrowed to his rigid abdomen. Another tattoo—this one a panther—was on his angular hip bone just above the rim of that towel. As thick and plush as that towel was, the lengthy member that hung between his thighs was clearly outlined.

She recalled the first time they kissed and she felt it press into her body with importance. *Uhm, uhm, uhm . . .*

"Listen, I was just about to make me something to eat. Wanna join me?"

She didn't want to go back to that house. Not yet. Dinner with a handsome man was a good reason not to return. She needed the time to process the fact that her father had broken his word to her yet again.

She felt comfortable around Kahron. Although she wasn't one hundred percent sure he wasn't behind sabotaging the ranch, she wasn't one hundred percent sure that he was, either. Maybe tonight she could get some insight to the man. Maybe she could pick up some clues to his involvement. Maybe she could just enjoy his company after he comforted her through an emotional breakdown.

"No, I'm gone head home," she said instead. She had to stop running from her drama with her father.

Kahron locked those hawklike eyes on her. "You can trust me, Bianca," he told her after long moments where his eyes perused hers.

Bianca licked her full lips and tilted her head to the side a bit as she looked at him. "My gut says the same thing," she admitted softly, even as she shrugged.

He pulled her into his arms and Bianca tilted her head back for the kiss she knew he was going to bless her with. She wasn't disappointed. Her arms snaked around his waist as his lips touch down upon hers again and again and again.

They moaned as they deepened it. They kissed each other with a tender yet passionate groove that left them both trembling.

"Aaah, you are so damn sexy, Kahron Strong," Bianca admitted against his lips before dropping her head to rest lightly against his chest. "But I gotta go before I jump all over you again."

Kahron nodded and released her with reluctance. "Let me take you to dinner," he offered, a smile at the corner of his mouth.

Bianca stepped back from him and felt the loss of his body's warmth. "I'm so busy with the ranch. Some other drama going on right now. I, uhm . . . I don't know. Let me think about it, okay?"

"Offer stands."

"Duly noted."

"You've struck me down twice."

"Third time's the charm."

"Duly noted as well."

"You don't have to walk me out," she told him as she moved to the door and pulled it open.

Hershey jogged into the room and looked between Bianca and her master.

When she looked back over her shoulder Kahron was standing with his hands on his hips, his erection clearly tenting the towel. He had the nerve to wink.

All Bianca could do was fan herself as she closed the door behind her.

Hank sat in his study. The room was dark as midnight, save for the lamp on the corner of his desk. The house was quiet. Papa Doc had gone on home and Trishon was upstairs watching television.

It was just him and his demons.

He licked his lips as he pulled the bottle of gin closer to him. He craved it. He needed it.

A vision of the look on Bianca's face tonight stopped him from opening it.

He truly loved his little girl. He hadn't meant to run her away. He needed her and he was glad she was home.

You need the booze more.

"No," he roared at his innermost thoughts, knocking the bottle down with his hand.

It fell and then spent, slowly coming to a stop with the cap of bottle facing him.

His mouth watered and his hands shook.

I promise you I will fix this but I need my Daddy. I need you to be the man you were before Mama died. It's either that liquor or me and this ranch. The choice is yours.

When his wife died a piece of him died with her and the rest he kept numb with booze. He knew he was wrong to rely on Bianca to pick up his slack as he drank away the pain of losing his wife. He knew that, but the liquor made him uncaring.

His breathing became shallow and his heart pumped furiously as his eyes bore into that bottle that seemed to mock him, call to him, complete him.

He wanted it so badly.

It's either that liquor or me and this ranch. The choice is yours.

He really tried to stop. He did. But the cravings overrode his rationale.

His business was in a shambles. His relationship with his daughter strained. His life a mess.

The look in her eyes tonight burned a hole through his soul.

I need my Daddy.

Hank began to weep.

Bianca entered the house and was headed up the stairs when she heard a noise from the study. She turned and headed that way. As she came to the open door, she saw her father sitting with his head down on the desk. Her eyes didn't miss the bottle of alcohol.

Vaguely she noted it was full as she walked into the room, flipping up the switch by the door to bask it with light. Her father's head rose and she saw the tears wetting his face. She wasn't moved. As a child she had been spectacle to many a drunken weep fest.

"We had a deal," she began in a cold voice—a mask to the pain she felt. "Why shouldn't I pack up and leave you here in this mess you call a life? I have my own business. My own home. A good life in Atlanta. Why . . . am . . . I . . . here?"

Hank wiped his face with his beefy hands. "I need you."

Bianca frowned. "You haven't needed me since Mama died."

"It was hard for me when she died, Bianca."

"Yes, but I didn't die with her."

The room became silent.

Bianca walked to the bar and picked up two glasses, bringing them back to the desk as she took a seat. "Do you think I loved my mother like you?" she asked, as she picked up the bottle, opened it, and poured the liquor into the glasses.

Hank looked confused. "Of course you did."

"Do you think I miss her like you?" Bianca asked as she set one glass in front of him and the other in front of herself.

"I know you do."

"Then how come only you get to numb the pain by being a drunk?" Bianca asked bitterly. "Let's both cop out and take the easy road. Drink up. We'll be two drunks together."

"Don't play with me, Bianca."

She picked up her glass and raised it in toast as she locked her eyes with his. "Who's playing?"

Hank reached out and knocked the glass from Bianca's hand, sending the glass flying across the room and some of the liquor into her lap.

He covered his face with both his hands. "I need help, Bianca. I can't . . . I can't . . . do it."

Bianca's heart broke at his admission. She rose and walked around the desk to gather him into her strong arms. "Then help is what you'll get, Daddy. I promise."

Bianca closed the brochures from the Oceanfront Clinic that she was reading. It was a pretty name for the upscale and exclusively private rehab center located in Hilton Head. It was her father's home—and she hoped his haven—during his reocvery. One hour ago Trishon and she returned after getting him settled at the facility, which looked more like a resort community.

Once her father asked for the help, Bianca got on the phone with a psychologist friend of hers back in Atlanta, and he had immediately recommended the Oceanfront Clinic. She called their twenty-four-hour hotline and was able to get him admitted immediately. After giving her father some private time to clue his wife in, Bianca had been more than anxious to make the hour-long ride that same night.

That man she left in that facility was but a shell of her father. She hoped she would recognize him again when his inpatient treatment was completed.

For now, well, for now she had to support her father through his rehabilitation, continue her efforts to at least *tolerate* Trishon—who grated her last nerve—and start her plan to get his business back on track.

Suddenly any plans to move back to Holtsville were firm. She still had to decide what to do with her practice. She wasn't sure if she would close it or sell it to the two vets she had on staff—if either were interested. Or she could just open a South Carolina office and keep her stake in the one in Atlanta. Decisions still to be made.

She set the catalogs atop her stack of *Equine Veterinary Journal*s before she turned off the lights and huddled under the satiny covers on her side. As was normal of late, as soon as her eyes closed she thought of Kahron. This time he was naked in a bathtub filled with whipped cream and it was her duty—and her pleasure— to lick every delicious inch of him clean. And she meant *every* inch.

She slept and dreamt for about an hour before something disturbed her sleep. Bianca hated that she was such a light sleeper.

She sat up in bed and looked around. Nothing seemed out of place, but the room was uncomfortably warm. She stretched and yawned as she flung back the covers and made her way to the window. She caught a glimpse of a dark, shadow crossing the front of the yard and disappearing into the bushes.

Bianca immediately thought of the vandalism and

wondered if it was the same criminal back to do more harm. She flew across the room and out the door, knowing she was acting like one of those idiot women in the movies who went looking for the boogeyman. Yeah, well she didn't know Kung Fu, but she knew plenty of crazy.

She paused at the top of the stairs at the sight of Trishon entering the house, still in her nightgown. "Trishon? What's going on?"

The other woman turned slowly as if it was the most natural thing in the world for her to be outside at 10 P.M. in her nightgown. She waved her hand, nonchalant. "My baby brother come to get some food again. You know how my people are."

Bianca's brows furrowed as Trishon continued up the stairs. "This time of the night?"

"I never wanted Hank to know I was sneaking them food, that's all. So they always come when Hank's not here or when they think he's sleeping."

Trishon reached the top of the stairs and she paused to stand beside Bianca, lightly patting her hand. "Why you up so late? Couldn't sleep?"

Bianca felt an uneasiness fill her and she couldn't explain it as she removed her hand from underneath Trishon's cool grasp. "I was going down to get some water," she lied.

"Well I'm beat. It's been a long day and without Hank I know I'm gone toss and turn all night, girl."

Bianca watched Trishon until she disappeared into her bedroom. She continued downstairs because she was up and made her way to the kitchen for that glass of water anyway. She dismissed her uneasiness to a case of the creeps.

She felt the hairs on the back of her neck stand on end

again and she turned to find Trishon standing on the stairs watching her. "Can I help you with something, Trishon?" Bianca asked.

She continued down the stairs. "I just thought we should have a girl chat about Kahron," Trishon said, as she moved into the room and took a seat at the island.

"Haven't we had this little chat already?" Bianca asked, as she took a deep sip of her water.

Trishon smiled. "But you're not taking me seriously."

"Why do you say that?" Bianca asked.

"I just don't want to see you hurt."

"Like Shauna, right?"

"Exactly."

Bianca said nothing else.

"I even hear he has a child in Summerville he don't claim."

Bianca poured the rest of her water into the sink and quickly washed her glass before setting it into the dish rack.

"And I've heard he's on powder."

Bianca turned slowly and faced Trishon. "Anything else?" she asked, her annoyance evident.

"Nothing you wanna hear."

"Well, that's funny because I didn't want to hear any of it, but I did." Bianca dried her hands with a piece of paper towel as she walked past Trishon and out the kitchen. "If you're finished with your version of *The National Enquirer* I'm going to bed."

"But he's—"

"Goodnight, Trishon," Bianca sang as she climbed the stairs.

Bianca closed the door of her bedroom and climbed between the purple satin covers. Trishon's admonitions about Kahron rolled off her back like water. She had already decided not to pursue anything with Kahron—no matter how tempting—and thus small town gossip was of no importance of her.

The charming thing about a small town was that everybody knew everybody and the bad thing about a small town was that everybody like *talking* about everybody.

Bianca reached to turn off the lavender crystal lamp on the nightstand. One thing she knew for sure, if Trishon cornered her one more time about Kahron the woman was going to explain just why *she* was so concerned.

7

"Sign here, ma'am."

Bianca accepted the clipboard from the delivery man, signing her name with flourish. "Thanks so much," she said, her eyes bright with pleasure as she handed him a tip.

"No problem."

Bianca watched as the man began to unload the crates of supplies from the rear of his truck. "You can just set them right here," Bianca said, pointing to a spot by the site where the steel barn was currently being erected.

Things were moving pretty smoothly and Bianca was glad for that. Jamison Contractors, Inc., a local company, was erecting the steel barn, and she'd hired two hands so far who were busy repairing and painting the wooden fence surrounded the perimeter of the property. A gentleman from the light company was installing tall night poles around the property—she hoped to deter anymore late night pranks.

There was much more to be done. Her intention was to hire at least two additional hands. The barn should be complete within a week, but she had not lined up any horse boarders yet. She had purchased three one-year-olds from North Carolina and, once delivered next month, they would be trained and, she hoped, sold locally. She was also in the process of contacting previous clients to woo their services back—and she thanked the heavens that the responses were more good than bad.

Bianca was surprised that so many people were well aware of her veterinary career in Atlanta. They were all proud of their hometown girl, and it touched Bianca that although she had left home so many people were glad for her return.

"You really got things moving."

Bianca turned at the sound of Papa Doc's voice, and she smiled in welcome as he left the cab of his bright red Dooley and walked toward her. "I mean business," she told him playfully, as he hugged her warmly to his side.

"How's your Daddy?" he asked.

"He's enjoying his vacation," Bianca said, shifting her eyes to the construction site.

"I know he's in detox, Bianca," he told her.

She looked up at him briefly.

"Trishon told me. I'm family. You don't have to lie to me."

Bianca nodded. "I know. Just trying to outrace that small town gossip. It can spread quicker than the clap in a whorehouse."

Papa Doc chuckled as he stuck his thumbs in the belt loops of his jeans. "Let me ask you though. You don't think this might not be too much for your Daddy to handle while he's trying to get sober."

Bianca frowned as she shaded the sun from her eyes with her hand. "What do you mean?"

"Well, I think part of the reason your Daddy went to drinking was trying to run this business. Stress can turn a man to vices."

Bianca remained quiet.

"I know you're all revved up to see this place back up and running, but don't forget your Daddy in all this."

"You saying I'm selfish?" Bianca asked, not trying to hide the indignation from her voice.

"No, I'm saying your Daddy's getting older and maybe he's not as interested as you are in all this. Hell, look at me, I used to work right along side him with them horses. You know that. I'm getting older and wrangling with a wild steer ain't in my blood like it used to be."

"I hear what your saying Papa Doc, but my Daddy called me home to get the job done," she told him, turning to look up into his broad face. "And that's what I'm gonna do."

"What about when you're gone back to Atlanta? Huh, then what?"

"Don't sound like you have a lot of faith in your friend?" Bianca said, not bothering to explain that she was seriously considering moving back to Holtsville.

Papa Doc put his hand on Bianca's shoulder and squeezed it warmly. "Don't take nothing I say the wrong way. I'm looking out for Hank is all."

"So am I, Papa Doc," she told him, warmth in her tones.

"Just listen to what I'm saying."

"I will."

He squeezed her shoulder one last reassuring time before he turned and got back into his truck. Bianca waved to him as he steered the truck up toward the main house.

She didn't have time to ponder Papa Doc's words as her cell phone rang from her back pocket. "Dr. Bianca King."

"Hey, when are you coming home *off* the range, sweetie?"

Bianca smiled at the sound of Mimi's voice. "Do you miss me, Mimi?" Bianca asked, dropping easily into her role as the straight man to Mimi's humor.

"Yes. I need my daily fill of pet stories from hell, darling," Mimi drawled.

Bianca climbed up onto the fence circling the daily turn out area. "I told you I was here for another two weeks or so," Bianca said.

"Oh heavens, Sweetie, you were serious?"

"Yes, I may even move home for good."

"Oh, Jesus, hold on a sec, 'kay?"

Bianca looked up and saw Hershey sitting on the hill above her. Her heart stopped. Seconds later it came back full force as Kahron came into view.

This was the first she'd seen of the handsome rascal in a week and she was honestly glad to see him. From the huge grin on his face, he was glad to see her as well.

"Yeah, Sweetie, I'm back, you're little news was cause for a double."

"Mimi, you ever been around a man who makes you forget rhyme and reason?" Bianca asked, her eyes absorbing everything about the man, the sun glinting from his hair, those aviators shading his eyes. His gait. His sexiness. His confidence.

"Yeah, seven times, remember?" Mimi asked, followed by a hysterical laugh.

Bianca released a low whistle of pure appreciation.

"He's right there isn't he? I can hear your noony-nack singing, Sweetie."

"Yes, and I will call you back."

"Keep your skirts down and your panties up, sweetie."

"Are you serious?" Bianca asked in disbelief.

"Yes, and celibate."

"Now, I *know* you lying."

Bianca closed the phone.

Kahron smiled up at her as he came to stand between her open legs. "Hi, stranger."

"Hi, Kahron. Where have you been keeping yourself?" she asked, and then hated when his eyes took on an all-too-knowing look.

"We had the cattle drive. Me and the men just got back today."

Bianca felt relief that his interest had not waned like she thought. "Not tired?" she asked, knowing how much hard work went into moving an entire herd of cattle to a new area of land.

"Very. I wanted to see you."

"I'm here working hard myself," she said.

Kahron looked around at the activity. "I must admit it's good to see the land not going to waste," he admitted. "You're really getting it done, huh?"

Bianca assessed him with her eyes, knowing how badly he wanted the land. "I'm determined to get it done. It *will* be done."

Kahron met her eyes. He looked like he wanted to say something.

"Say it," she urged.

"This is all well and good, but what's gonna happen when you go back to Atlanta."

"Who said I'm going back for good?" she admitted softly. He was the first person in Holtsville that she gave a hint of her plans. She hadn't even told her father yet.

His face became bright with pleasure. "That's something I don't mind being wrong about."

"Oh really?"

Kahron nodded. "Just admit you missed me."

"How can I miss you when I don't even know you?" she retorted, although that was a lie. She looked up every day hoping to see him. When she went to the store she looked to see if he was around.

He reached up and placed one strong hand on each of her thighs. "Let's get to know each other."

His hands were warm—even through her jeans. Never had she been so acutely aware of a man, and to Bianca that meant something.

She tilted her head to the side and reached out to remove his shades. With a soft smile she looked into those eyes and saw twin reflections of herself looking at him adoringly. "Ask me again," she said softly, knowing her request needed no further explanation.

Kahron moved his hands up to grasp her sides lightly as he stepped closer to her. He tilted his head up and licked his lips, seeming a bit nervous. "Bianca King, will you go to dinner with me?"

Bianca cut her eyes up to the sky and placed her finger to her mouth. "Let me see . . ."

"You little tease," he said, easily picking her up by her waist.

Bianca squealed a little, bringing her hands down to rest on each of his broad shoulders.

Kahron let his hands circle around her until his arms were wrapped around her just under her buttocks. He began to spin with a huge and handsome grin on his face.

Hershey wanted to get in on their play and she rose to bark noisily and circle them.

"Okay, okay. Yes. Yes," Bianca screamed.

Kahron stopped and loosened the grip of his arms so that her body slid down the length of his until her face was aligned with his. He felt their heart pounding in unison as he kissed her briefly, but with warm and enticing pleasure.

Bianca wrapped her arms around his strong neck as

she felt happy for the first time in a long time. This man brought her joy and she didn't want to deny herself that feeling. "Dressy or casual?"

"Oh definitely dressy. I want to see you in something besides jeans."

Hershey sat and watched them, her tongue wagging heavily and wetly from her open mouth.

"I think we have an audience," Kahron whispered.

Bianca looked beyond Kahron's head and saw that nearly every man on the property was openly staring at them.

Now men gossiped just as much as women—if not more—and Bianca knew that for a fact. So news of their spectacle would make it to the dinner tables and porches of every available home this very evening. The power of informal communication was legendary.

Kahron let Bianca down and she wiped the faint taste of him from her lips. "What time should I be ready?" she asked.

"Seven."

"Okay."

He reached up to squeeze the tip of her nose lightly before turning and walking away, Hershey quickly at his heels.

Bianca picked up her cell phone that she had dropped somewhere along the line. She was glad that the men had all gone back to their task. She had to fight to keep from smiling like a fool because she was excited—more so than she had been in along time—about the night ahead.

"You full of shit, Kahron Strong."

He looked up to see Trishon walking down the porch of the house toward him. "Good afternoon to you too, Trishon."

"Why you sniffing around Bianca's tail so much?" she asked.

Kahron opened the tailgate so that Hershey could jump onto the back of the truck. He shot her a sidelong glance. "Mad because I never sniffed around yours?"

"I don't go throwing myself at half-naked men, thankyouverymuch."

"No, you just marry old men for money,"

Trishon's mouth tightened as her eyes flashed. "Hank King is more man than you'll ever be, Kahron Strong."

"Who you trying to convince, me or you?" He climbed into his truck, sliding his shades back into place before he drove away without another word.

Bzzzzz.

He stepped away from the crowd of people surrounding him as his cell phone vibrated against his hip. He removed it from the clip and looked down at a number that he knew so well. Assured no one could here him, he answered. "Speak."

"She's ruining everything," the voice chewed out in obvious anger. "If she had stayed her ass in Atlanta everything woulda worked out like we planned."

"What do you want me to do?"

He listened to their instructions, pressing the phone closer to his ear with eagerness.

"Done deal," he replied, closing the phone and slipping it back onto the clip on his hip.

"Wow, you look beautiful."

Bianca smiled in pleasure as she spun on the center of the porch, causing the intricately beaded skirt she wore to flare up around her thighs like a parasol. She had put a lot of time into her appearance and she wanted just this reaction from Kahron.

"You looking good yourself," she told him as she slowly moved down the stairs toward where he stood next to a vintage-looking car in a beautiful shade of silver.

Kahron wore a crisp white shirt beneath a navy tailored blazer that fit loosely on his frame and fit him well. His vintage jeans and boots gave him the perfect look. "Just a little something, something I threw together," he joked as he took her hand and led her around to the passenger side of the car with its classic long hood and scooped fenders.

"Wow, this is nice." Bianca slid onto the leather seating after he shut the door.

Kahron came around to slide into the driver's seat. "This is my baby," he told her with eagerness as he turned the key in the ignition. The car purred to life with ease. "I restored her myself about three years ago."

Bianca tilted her head and smiled over at him. "So you're good with your hands?" she asked huskily.

A slow and satisfying grin spread across his face. "Damn good," he answered with emphasis.

"I believe it."

Kahron leaned forward and tasted her lips with a short moan of pleasure. The soft, fine hairs of his shadow lightly tickling her skin.

Bianca settled back against her seat, leaning a little toward Kahron as she enjoyed the comfortable intimacy of the car. "I used to have a playhouse in those woods," she told him as they slowly crept up the dirt road leading from the ranch.

Kahron turned and smiled at her. "Life was simple when we were kids."

"Nothing to do but play. We had it good and didn't even know it."

Kahron settled in his seat as he turned the vehicle onto the main road and accelerated forward. He reached over and gathered Bianca's hand into his own. "Growing up on a working cattle ranch we had chores as soon as we could walk and were potty trained."

Bianca looked at him in disbelief.

"Okay, maybe not that soon, but I just remember always being busy."

Bianca enjoyed the feel of Kahron's thumb circling the back of her hand. "Does your family still ranch?"

"My father and oldest brother, Kade, still operate Strong Ranch in Walterboro. My brother, Kaleb, runs a dairy ranch. Now my younger brother, Kaeden, is everyone's business manager—he's an accountant. And Kaitlyn, well she's busy being twenty and giving my mother more gray hairs."

"You all are very close?" Bianca asked, turning her head to look out at the dark shadows of the trees lining the road. Maybe if she had siblings, she wouldn't have suffered through her father's emotional distance after her mother's death.

"Yeah, we all meet up to my parents for a big dinner every Sunday, and any holiday, birthday, or major announcement is cause for one of my mama's barbeques."

"I would love to have a big family one day," she admitted.

Kahron squeezed her hand as he steered the vehicle up Highway 17 toward Charleston. "I'm working on it."

Bianca warmed at the thought of a son with Kahron's devilish grin, but she said, "Let's get through this first date, okay?"

"You know you want me to be your baby-daddy."

Bianca just laughed before they settled into a comfortable silence. "You don't have any kids, do you?" Bianca asked, hating that she let Trishon's gossip intrude on her date.

"Definitely not, and not even the one in Summerville everyone says is mine."

Bianca dropped her eyes guiltily when he cast her a knowing glance.

"Can I assume Trishon filled you in on my supposed sins?"

Bianca said nothing.

"And this from a woman who doesn't even associate with her family. She acts like her own mother doesn't exist."

"That doesn't surprise me," Bianca said.

"Bianca, I am not the kind of man who wouldn't claim his children," he told her, as he pulled the car up to a red light. "I wasn't even dating the girl when she got pregnant. We hadn't been together for at least five or sixths months before that."

"That's none of my business, Kahron."

"Any other rumors you want to dispel?" he asked, humor in his raspy voice.

"As a matter of fact, yes."

His look was questioning.

Bianca reached up and stroked his beard. "I heard that you were one hella good kisser." She leaned forward to press her lips to his with a soft purr, nibbling his bottom lip before she traced his lips with her clever tongue.

Kahron took the lead, leaning forward to capture her tongue with his own intimately. His hands left the steering wheel to rest warmly on her thigh as the intensity of their kisses increased and the steam rose from their bodies.

Bianca slid her hand up to his nape as she pressed his head closer.

Kahron's hand rose to her hip and his fingers pressed into the silk of her camisole as he lightly massaged the curve as he drew her tongue into his cool mouth to suckle deeply.

The sound of someone leaning on their horn broke them apart. Their shallow breathing echoed in the car. Bianca's taut nipples throbbed to be touched, stroked, and suckled as they pressed against the thin material of her lace bra and camisolelike twin pebbles.

Kahron accelerated forward, the light long since green. He shifted in his seat, rising a bit to loosen the material around his obvious erection. "How'd I do?"

Bianca inched her skirt up a little around her knees as she used her purse to fan playfully between her legs. "Damn good," Bianca sighed, letting her head fall back against the headrest. "Oh yeah."

"I am stuffed," Bianca sighed rubbing her stomach as they enjoyed a relaxing stroll along historic Waterfront Park.

"That was all those croissant rolls you ate," Kahron teased. "You ate more of them than you did your dinner."

They enjoyed dinner at California Dreaming on Ashley River, the only restaurant in Charleston where every table had an excellent waterfront view of the harbor.

"I'm a carb junkie."

"I'm a meat man myself."

Bianca cast him a sidelong glance. "I'm sure you are."

Kahron wiggled his brows suggestively, placing his arm comfortably around her shoulders.

They continued along the waterfront, other couples also strolling and enjoying the view of the moonlight sky against the deep darkness of the water. Charleston Waterfront Park was a twelve-acre park located along the Cooper River. There was a four-hundred-foot-long wharf and a fishing pier with shade structures, a riverside promenade, lawns and formal gardens, tree-shaded walking and seating areas, and two major fountains that were exquisite in design.

Kahron and Bianca came to a stop at the park main entrance near a fountain surrounded by decorative walls with ornamental iron fencing. Kahron leaned back against the wall and pulled Bianca back against him, his arms circling loosely around her waist. He enjoyed the feel of her body next to his.

"I'm having such a nice time." Bianca let her head fall back against Kahron's broad shoulder as her fingers covered his. "I don't want the night to end."

Kahron leaned his face against Bianca's, his nose flaring as he inhaled deeply of her scent. "Me either. I could hold you in my arms like this forever."

Bianca turned and pressed her face into his neck as she let her eyes drift close. "I don't want you to let me go."

Kahron kissed her temple.

Bianca was such a unique woman to him. She was smart, driven, focused, courageous, and sexy. His heart raced when she smiled and she made him hard as stone with her touch. There was a connection between them that seemed natural and right.

She made him laugh. When she gave in to the carefree side of herself Bianca had the kind of dry humor that made your sides ache with laughter.

She made him think. The woman had an opinion on everything from politics to pop culture. She was impassioned about her views, but she also wanted to know what he thought about things. Was he as angry as she over the treatment of the New Orleans residents after Hurricane Katrina? What did he think about the war? Poverty? Racism? Gross consumption? The portrayal of women in hip-hop? It felt good to converse with a woman whose topics weren't limited to fashion or other inane subjects.

She impressed him. Kahron visited the website of her clinic and the accolades that she was too humble to mention were listed there. Now, the way she had taken on the challenge of revitalizing her father's business let him know the woman was amazing.

She made him happy. Sitting across from Bianca as she affectionately caressed his hand and gave him her full attention pleased him and made him want to please her. To see a smile on her face and in her eyes made his heart swell in his chest.

She made him want to prove that she could trust him. He knew she had had doubts about his involvement in the sabotage of her father's business, but here she was giving him the benefit of the doubt. To him, that was major.

He hadn't felt this strongly about a woman in a long time and never this quickly.

"I could see myself falling in love with you, Bianca King," he admitted as he rubbed his beard lightly against the side of her face.

She tilted her head back and looked up at him. "And I'd fall right along with you," she answered him huskily, the truth of her words in her hazel-green eyes.

8

Bianca didn't think life could get much better.

Her father was in rehab to help him learn to battle his alcoholism. She had the ranch on track for a future grand re-opening. Last night she welcomed Kahron into her life, her world, her heart.

Oh, she didn't love him—they'd only had one date—but she *wanted* to love him, so she would offer no resistance.

She stretched in the bed, wishing Kahron was laying there beside her. He was busy on his ranch all day and she was driving into Walterboro to run some errands and start apartment hunting, but they had plans to have dinner at his house later that night.

Her cheeks flushed as she recalled the last time she'd been to Kahron's house. She'd jumped on him like white in rice. She could only shake her head in shame as she climbed out of bed.

Bianca was showered, dressed in a casual velour sweatsuit, and heading downstairs in an hour. She didn't see Trishon and was glad. The woman's attempts at souring her on Kahron were not going to ruin her good mood.

She left the house and climbed into her vehicle, pushing

the button to lower the convertible top. She tooted her horn as she passed Papa Doc and Dante, one of Kahron's ranch hands, talking at the store. They both waved back at her as she whizzed up Highway 17, the sounds of Alicia Keys blaring from her speakers.

When his ranch manager, Carlos Santos, came to Kahron and suggested that he hire his youngest daughter, Garcelle, as his new housekeeper/cook, Kahron had been reluctant. With his luck Garcelle might turn out to be a real piece of work and when Kahron fired her that might anger Carlos—leading him to quit.

When Carlos stressed that the income would allow Garcelle to save for college, however, which was something she desperately wanted to do, Kahron's kind-hearted nature won out. He just hoped he wouldn't regret his decision.

"Mister Strong . . . Mister Strong!"

Kahron turned from brushing down Midnight to see Paco running toward him. "Whassup, Paco?"

"My sister said to tell you your lunch is ready," Paco said, grinning up at him as he shook the hair from his eyes.

His stomach grumbled loudly. "Tell her I'm on my way."

He watched as Paco went running back toward the main house before he finished grooming Midnight and then leading her to her stall. He had just gotten back from checking on the herd and he was starving.

Kahron climbed onto the four wheeler, laughing as Hershey rose to run behind him as he headed for the house. Paco was sitting on the porch reading a book when Kahron pulled up.

"Paco, will you feed Hershey for me?" Kahron asked as he climbed the stairs.

"Sure thing, Mister Strong."

The grumbling of Kahron's stomach increased as he entered the house. Whatever Garcelle was cooking smelled divine and he hoped it tasted as well. No matter how it tasted it felt good to come home and smell real food being cooked.

He was headed to the kitchen when he noticed that his living room was spotless. Gone were the magazines, old dinner plates, and dirty clothing that had littered the floor. Even the stain in the carpet from when he accidentally kicked over a glass of fruit punch was gone. The fine layer of dust that accumulated quickly on the furniture was absent. The windows were open and the summer breeze filtered into the house.

Kahron did a quick walk through of the house. His bedroom and private bathroom was spotless as well. Even the small clutter he made this morning was absent, and the faint scent of something lemony filled the rooms.

Kahron was impressed.

Garcelle did more in three hours than all the other housekeepers had ever did . . . combined.

He made his way back up the hall and to the right towards the kitchen. The scent of the food strengthened and Kahron's steps quickened.

Garcelle turned and smiled at him as she held a plate in her hands. Kahron was caught a little off guard. This was his first time meeting Garcelle, and she was quite pretty. *Very* pretty in fact. Long jet black hair. A smooth brown complexion. The striking, yet angelic features of Beyonce—with the body to match.

Okay, she's fine. Duly noted. Now move on, you have Bianca. His heart raced at the thought of Bianca and he knew her place in his life was not threatened. Although he had to wonder what *she* would think about his new housekeeper. Was she the insecure, jealous type—like Shauna—or would she take it in all in stride and know that she could trust him—even with a beautiful woman floating around his home.

Garcelle would in fact be a good test of Bianca's faith in him.

"It's nice to meet you, Señor Strong. And thank you again for giving me the job," she said, her Spanish accent very pronounced.

"Your very welcome," Kahron said, moving to take a seat at the table. "Boy, this smells good."

"Everyone loves *quesadilla*," she said, moving back over to the sink. "And I have made *paella* for your dinner. Just put it in the oven for thirty minutes when you come in this evening."

Kahron just nodded as he shoved one of the triangular slices of tortilla with melted cheese and stewed chicken in tomato sauce into his mouth. It was way better than the quesadilla appetizers he enjoyed at Ruby Tuesday or Applebee's, and, Lord knows, Taco Bell's offering was ridiculous in comparison.

Garcelle set a glass of lemonade next to his plate. "I'm going to the laundry room. Just holler if you need me."

Kahron waved her off as he took a large gulp of the lemonade—which he found to have a hint of lime and orange in it.

Had his luck finally changed when it came to housekeepers? He hoped so.

Kahron was browsing through the morning paper and finishing up his lunch when his cell phone vibrated against his hip. Wiping his hand against his dusty jeans to remove the grease, he answered it. "Strong here . . . hey Bianca—"

His face went from pleasure to anger and then concern. "I'm on my way."

Seconds later he was out the door and climbing into his pick-up truck headed to Walterboro.

Bianca felt heated with a blend of emotions.

Who would do such a thing? She wondered as she paced the length of the car in the parking lot outside of the new Super Wal-Mart. She wished she could get her hands *and* feet on the culprit. Her emotions ran the gamut. From helplessness to anger to fear and back again.

When she looked down and saw her beautiful Volvo sitting on all four rims—its deflated tires looking like sagging skin hanging from the metal—she felt like screaming, "*Why?*", at the top of her lungs; but because she wasn't that dramatic and she was sure people would stare even more than they already were, Bianca refrained. So, she paced as she awaited the police and Kahron to arrive.

Okay, Bianca admittedly wasn't playing the helpless female role, but she wasn't exactly the "I hate all men" kind of woman either. It felt good to have a man to call for help and he asked no questions, offered no excuses, and just said, "I'm on my way."

It felt *damn* good.

So, even as the police turned into the parking lot—the blue light sirens just a blaring like a murder had occurred—it was Kahron Bianca wanted as she tried to figure why someone had slashed her tires and dug the word *BITCH* into the paint.

Two policeman left their black and gold cruiser—one white and the other black—and walked toward her, frowning as they took in the sad sight her vehicle made.

The crowd that was milling about and gawking increased in size until a semi-circle surrounded her and the area where the police cruiser and her vehicle sat.

"How do you do, ma'am?" The tall police officer asked, his notepad and pen poised for action.

"I was doing just fine until I came outside and saw this," Bianca answered politely, waving her hand toward her car.

She maintained her patience through all of their questions—knowing that they were doing their job. And they asked many questions—so many that they started to blend one into the other.

In the end they were just as baffled to the cause for the vandalism, even suggesting it was a random crime.

"I thank you so much for your time, gentleman," Bianca told them.

"Shame to mess up a beauty like that," the short officer said.

"I would have been no less upset if it was hooptie," she assured them with honesty.

"Sure you don't need a ride home?" the brother, Officer Laskin, asked as he slid his notepad back into his pocket.

"No thank you my—"

Bianca paused. What was Kahron to her, certainly after one date she wasn't grouping him into the boyfriend category? It was far too soon for that, but nothing else seemed to fit.

"My friend," she finished. "He's on the way."

"Lucky man," the tall brother said, giving her an appreciative once over before he headed to his vehicle.

Just then, Bianca saw Kahron's truck turn into the parking lot. Her eyes stayed glued to the truck until he parked and walked through the crowd to reach her. He made an ugly face at the sight of her car before pulling her to his side with one strong arm.

Officer Laskin's face lit up in recognition. "Oh, hey whaddup, Kahron," he called over.

Kahron gave him the universal head nod for a greeting. "Whaddup, Danny."

"I called my insurance and they're sending a tow truck," Bianca told him as the cruiser pulled out the lot. "I just don't understand all the whos and whys of it all. The officers said it might be random."

"Considering you just got back in town, I would guess that's most likely what it is," Kahron added, rubbing his beard as his eyes pierced the vehicle.

"If it had happened on the ranch I would of thought it was the same creep who . . ."

Kahron faced became doubtful and that caused Bianca's words to trail off.

"You still don't think my father's ranch was vandalized at all do you?" she asked, crossing her arms over her chest as she looked at him in surprise.

Kahron's eyes shifted from hers.

Bianca swatted his arm. "Kahron!" she exclaimed in disbelief.

He looked at her helplessly with his hands open. "What?" he asked. "Listen, I just don't see what could be gained by any of it."

Bianca shook her head as if to clear it and then looked at him like he had two heads. "There was nothing to be gained by this—" she waved her hand at her car. "But *it* was done."

"You got a point and I'm sorry. Let's not turn on each other, B."

The tow truck pulled up and the big burly man with shocking red hair started working to load the vehicle.

Bianca picked up her hobo pocketbook and her bag from Wal-Mart from atop the rear of the car. She put her purse strap on her shoulder and slid her oversized shades onto her face.

Kahron took the bag from her hands as they walked over to his truck. Before Bianca could climb up onto the seat, Kahron turned her and pulled her against his warm and secure body.

Bianca wrapped her arms around him tightly, pressing her face against his chest as she inhaled deeply of his scent. It felt so good to have someone to lean on.

"Did you find an apartment?" Kahron asked as he stepped back to allow Bianca to enter the truck.

She heard Kahron speaking but her mind was elsewhere. She could gloss it over and fall into this man's arms and move on, but the point remained that someone had just slashed all four of her tires and then dug profanity into the paint. *What the hell*?

She leaned back into her seat, her eyes focused on some unknown point out the window. *Why?*

"Hey. Hey you."

Bianca turned her head to look at Kahron as he climbed into the truck with ease. "Huh?" she asked softly.

"Never mind," he said, starting the car.

Bianca reached across the seat for his hand, entwining their fingers. "I'm sorry. I guess I just don't feel like talking right now."

"Understandable."

They rode home in silence.

Bianca wrestled with her emotions as she stroked the side of Kahron's strong hand with her thumb. As they entered Holtsville, Bianca noticed Papa Doc's big truck still parked at the store.

"Papa Doc told me he's retired," Bianca asked suddenly. "What does he do for money?"

"Just what you see him doing now," Kahron drawled. "He gets a pretty good disability check from when he was in the military. Why?"

Bianca shrugged a little. "Just curious."

"Wanna come out to the ranch?" he asked, looking over at her.

"Actually, I got some things I want to check back at Daddy's."

Kahron nodded.

"My father's in detox," she admitted to him softly.

Kahron's faced registered surprise. "Now *that's* good news," he said with pleasure, squeezing her hand. "For how long."

"Thirty days."

"My daddy used to brag on how even the richest white farmers would take their horses to Hank King for training," Kahron said. "Your daddy's was a legend in these parts. Straight up, Bianca? It was a damn shame to see how liquor just knocked him down. It was a waste, you know?"

"I really want to help him," Bianca stressed, turning her head to look at him.

Kahron turned his head to look at her as well, his eyes serious. "Now that I know he's trying to kick the booze I think you can help him."

"I guess that's why I want to move home. He's my father. My Daddy, you know. And . . . I . . . want him in my life. I don't want to look back anymore, or he passes on—God forbid—and I didn't have him in my life."

Kahron squeezed her hand.

"Family is more important than a big house in Atlanta

or a practice." Bianca released a heavy breath. "I've missed my Daddy so much," she finished with emotion.

"You feel guilty about leaving, don't you?" he asked softly, raising their entwined hands to his mouth.

Bianca licked her lips and shifted her eyes to look out the window as they filled with shame. "Yes," she admitted softly, so softly that it sounded more like a release of air than a word.

"Well, you shouldn't feel guilty. You did what you had to do, Bianca," he stressed. "Maybe now you both can make it up to each other."

She turned her head to look at him with a soft smile. "You know what, you're right."

"Well, you know, what can I say," he said, imitating J.J. from the Seventies sitcom, *Good Times*.

Bianca laughed as he steered the truck down the dirt road leading to the ranch. The interior of the truck darkened by the shade offered by the trees. "Stop," Bianca said suddenly.

Kahron looked left and right. "What? What's wrong?

"Nothing, just pull on the side," she told him, slipping her hand from his.

Kahron did as she bid.

As soon as the truck stopped, Bianca jumped out of the truck. "Come on," she told him, swinging the door closed.

Kahron looked doubtful. "Come where?"

Bianca winked at him. "If you scared, say you scared," she told him flippantly, before continue on between the tree trunks.

She didn't doubt he would follow as she continued forward looking for the little spot where she used to play as a child in her magical forest. She heard Kahron's footsteps behind her and she continued on until she heard the gentle running of the tiny stream. Her steps quickened.

She sighed with pleasure as she broke through the bushes. The grass on either side of the tiny stream was as green as emeralds. There was a tiny break in the trees where just the hint of the blue sky and the rays of the sun broke through.

Bianca kicked off her sneakers and dug her toes into the grass, just as Kahron's strong arm circled her waist. "Beautiful isn't it?" she asked, turning to wrap her arms around his strong neck.

Kahron pushed his shades up onto his head as he held her with one arm. "Damn, who knew this was here," he said, looking around almost in wonder.

"I found it when I was a child and I never told a soul, not even my father," Bianca said, smiling on the memories. "It was my special place."

It was quiet and peaceful, nothing but the gentle running of the stream made a sound.

Bianca tilted her head up and lightly tasted Kahron's lips. He brought his other hand up to rest on the curve of her waist. She kissed him again, letting her eyes close. Kahron deepened the kiss with a moan.

Bianca pressed every curve of her luscious body against him as his tongue circled her own with skillful ease. She reached behind her for his hands and brought them up to the sides of her body to grasp each of her breasts warmly through the T-shirt she wore. Bianca gasped hotly, her breath fanning against his face, as his fingers moved to lightly stroke and pluck her taut and swollen nipples. "Yes," she moaned, shifting her lips to suck his neck lightly. She reveled in the shiver she felt course over his body.

Kahron let Bianca's upper body drape over his arm as

he used one hand to raise her T-shirt up above her breasts. The sheer lace of her black bra did nothing to hide her nipples from his eager eyes. Still, he raised the bra as well.

Raising his arm he brought Bianca's body closer to him, bending to take one full breast into his mouth. The faint scent of her perfume teased him as he lightly drew circles around the taut nipples before drawing it deeply into his mouth to suckle.

Bianca cried out in sweet, torturous desire.

Kahron felt his penis lengthen and harden as he flickered the chocolate tip with his tongue in rapid, feather-light motions that made her squirm in his arms. "Feels good?" he asked, his eyes open and watching her as he continued the light flickering.

Bianca grunted softly in pleasure. "Yes," she moaned.

Kahron laughed huskily, sending cool breath against her moist nipples.

Bianca raised her arms and tugged the shirt and bra over her head to drop to the thick grass beneath them. She rose and pressed her upper body to Kahron's, wishing he was as bare-chested as she. "This is the perfect place to make love," she said softly as she began to unbutton his shirt with trembling fingers and kiss each smooth piece of bronzed skin she exposed.

Kahron lifted his hands to Bianca, stopping her from her task.

She looked up at him, her face flushed with desire, her eyes clouded with want.

He took a deep breath, wondering if he was crazy. His penis was so hard and straining against the zipper of his pants that he thought he would come on himself just from wanting to be with her. "We can't do this. We're not ready."

Bianca waited for a better explanation why they

shouldn't take sweet advantage of such a peaceful and romantic place to make love for their first time. So she said nothing as she continued to look at him.

"I want this to be about more than sex between us, Bianca," he began. "I want to build something lasting with you."

"Me too, Kahron," she told him, looking up at him in innocence.

"So you understand why I think we should wait?"

"Not at all," Bianca answered, very no-nonsense as she began to unbutton his shirt again.

Kahron grimaced with pleasure as Bianca pulled his shirt opened and pressed her lips to his left nipple, rolling her tongue around it. He stepped back from her. "Sex complicates things," he told her, trying to hold true to his feelings about taking things slowly with Bianca because he wanted them to last. "I can't think straight I want you so much."

Bianca locked her eyes with his as she slid her sweatpants and bikinis over her hips to step out of. Naked and unashamed she enjoyed his eyes perusing her body, but she wanted to feel his touch.

Kahron took in everything. He thought a woman never looked so sexy as Bianca standing there naked before him, surrounding by nature. The cinnamon bronze of her skin. Her breasts full and heavy with large taut nipples he wanted to stoke. Her hips were wide and curvy with every bit of the natural curl surrounding the plump mound between her shapely thighs gone. Kahron heard nothing but the roar of his blood as it rushed to swell and lengthen his penis further.

She stepped closer to him. "Why think? Just do," she said softly, raising her hands to slide his shirt off his broad bronzed shoulders and down his arms.

Her very touch was like fire to him.

Bianca had never wanted anyone so much.

As she pressed her upper body to his, she lightly suckled his earlobe whispering, "I want to feel you inside me."

Kahron's resolve broke.

He would make sure they still talked and learned more about each other. He would never forget to romance her. He would still build a future with this amazing—and exhilarating—woman who captured a piece of him from the start. Sex would be a part of their relationship but not the whole sum of it.

But for now . . .

9

When Bianca finished undressing him, Kahron used their pile of discarded clothing to make a makeshift pallet for them. He lifted her easily into his arms before kneeling to lay her upon it. He shifted to kneel between her open legs, his erection hanging heavily and awkwardly between his thighs, throbbing with a beat all its own.

His heated eyes worshipped every warm curve of her frame, loving the way the moist and intricate folds of her core peeked through the darkened lips of the plump mound between her legs. His mouth literally watered to taste her intimately.

So he's gray all over, she thought with a soft smile as she took in the scattering of gray hair leading from his abdomen down to the flat and smooth hairs surrounding his hard and thick length. His penis was dark and almost furious in color as it curved near the smooth tip, causing one devilish-looking hook that she knew would miss not one inch of her core. She shivered with a slight moan. "I see you've been blessed," she sighed with pleasure as she bit her bottom lip.

Kahron smiled, taking his shaft into to his hand to

massage the full length of it before he tapped it lightly against her thigh with a solid *thump*.

Bianca leaned forward to take his hot penis into her hands, wanting to stimulate and pleasure him. She massaged the length of him with a steady rhythmic rubbing. Her touch was gentle but strong as she watched him closely.

Kahron flung his head back, rising up to press his hips forward, making the panther tattoo seem to jump forward at her as she continued to stroke him in that same slow and steady motion that made him want to come. "Damn," he swore, topping her hand with his own to stop her as he felt his seed about to spill. "I don't want to come."

"Not yet," Bianca agreed, sliding her free hand down her body to stroke the swollen and sensitive bud between her legs lightly.

She watched him with half-closed eyes as he watched her in open fascination. She eased her fingers away as she felt her release, squirming as her heart thundered in her chest.

Kahron picked up her hand and locked his eyes with hers boldly as he suckled the moistness from each of her fingers, enjoying the taste of her. He released her hand and leaned forward to kiss her everywhere. Her eyelids. Her cheeks. Her neck. Each taut plump nipple. The sides of her breasts. Arms. Shoulders. Stomach—where he circled her belly button with his tongue and then blew a cool stream of air against it, causing her to shiver. Her thighs. Her knees. Even her toes.

"Uhm, uhm, uhm." Bianca was breathless.

He rose up from her feet to use his hands to spread her thighs wider as he lay flat between her legs. The lips of her core were open to him and he lowered his head, inhaling deeply of her womanly scent before he used his tongue to draw her bud from the inner lips. He suckled it into his mouth once freed and had to lock his forearm around Bianca's fleshy brown thighs as her hips jerked up at the feel of his intimate kisses.

Kahron circled the bud with his tongue and just when Bianca thought she couldn't hold back cries of pleasures from bouncing into the forest, he slid his stiffened tongue inside of her.

She gasped out harshly, her back arching as he began to stroke her core with his tongue.

Kahron enjoyed the taste of her and the feel of her warmth surrounding his tongue, shifting it up briefly to flicker her bud, before plunging it inside of her again. He continued that devastating in and out motion before he began to suckle that bud in the same rhythmic way she stroked him.

Slow and steady. In and out.

Bianca squeezed her eyes shut as heat began to rise from her toes as she flung her head back and forth, her breath starting to come in gasps as Kahron pushed her to edge.

Slow and steady. In and out with a light sucking motion that was perfect. Absolutely perfect.

Kahron opened his eyes to look up at Bianca as he never broke his stride. Never changed the pace.

Slow and steady. In and out.

As he watched her like a hawk, she arched her back and clutched the blades of grass around her as she began to roll her hips up against his mouth. He wanted to make her come and finally release that scream of pleasure that she was holding back.

Slow and steady. In and out.

Bianca felt a delicious tingling course over her body

as her heart thundered. She felt sexy. Alive. Uninhibited. Exhilarated. *Free*. Her grasp of the grass loosened as she continued to roll her hips slowly, shifting her hand to grasp the back of his silver head. Kahron made her feel good deep in her core—but even deeper in her soul.

"Yes," she moaned softly, just louder than a whisper, feeling increasing excitement. "Yes . . . yes . . . yes . . . yes, yes, yes, yes, yes."

Kahron ached and throbbed to bury himself deep within her walls, but first—and most importantly to him—he wanted her to step through the door of ultimate release and just holler and let the woods around them absorb the sound. He knew it was near as he felt her bud warm and swell inside his mouth.

"Hmmmmmmmm," she sighed as the first white hot spasm of release caused her hips to jerk up roughly, her walls began to throb, and her clitoris to pulsate thickly like a heartbeat.

Slow and steady. In and out.

Lord, he's crucial. Bianca trembled from her thighs up. "I'm coming," she gasped, trying like hell to push Kahron's head away for fear she would pass out from pure unadulterated pleasure as her walls contracted.

Kahron deepened the sucking motion but not the pace.

Slow and steady. In and out.

She let out a sharp cry of ardor and release that she couldn't contain, her hips wildly thrusting up against his hot mouth. Time and place was lost as Bianca rode the waves and felt like she was free falling through air.

Kahron's assault continued even as the length of his shaft throbbed beneath him, a bit of his seed wetting the grass where he lay.

Slow and steady. In and out.

"Yes," she cried out roughly, wildly, wantonly.

Kahron closed his eyes as he suckled the whole of throbbing moist core into his mouth, devouring her juices as he tightened his grasps around her hips to keep her thrashing from freeing her bud from his grasp.

Bianca felt like she flying as tears filled her eyes.

Kahron felt the shiver of her body subside and he opened his eyes to see the wetness on Bianca's cheeks. With one final kiss to her pulsing lips, Kahron moved his body up to lay beside her and gather her into his arms as he kissed away the tracks of her tears.

"Good thing we're outside," he teased.

Bianca buried her face into his chest as she laughed. "Put Tarzan to shame."

She raised her head to look at him with a deadpan face. "Oh, you got jokes, huh?" she asked.

"Yup, and you got a set of lungs."

"*She* who laughs last, laughs best," she told him sultrily as her hands surrounded his shaft.

Kahron's eyes smoldered and darkened with immediate desire. "So what you saying?" he asked with mock bravado as she used one hand to push him down onto his back.

"Oh, it's on." Bianca straddled him, sitting on his strong thighs as she massaged him with both hands, long and swiftly, teasing the smooth thick tip.

Kahron eyes locked on the motion of her hands as he crossed his arms behind his head. "Damn, that feels good," he said throatily with a long intake of breath that sounded like a hiss.

Bianca wetly licked her hands from fingertips to palm and grasped him again. His hips jerked up from the earth. "Better, right?" she asked, saucily.

Kahron nodded.

"So you just laying back chillin', right?" she asked, slanting her head to look down at her handiwork.

He cut his eye up to her. "Just enjoying it, baby. Shit."

Bianca released him and stretched her entire body out atop his, her toes just reaching his ankles. "A perfect fit," she told him in that intimate space between them, as she looked down into his eyes.

"Damn right," he growled, reaching up to capture her lips with his own as his hands rose to squeeze each of her luscious buttocks firmly.

Bianca raised her hands to caress the sides of his face, his beard supple to her touch as she enjoyed the feel of his hardness pressing into her soft belly with power and dominance.

The mood between them shifted yet again, their playfulness fading into the heated steam rising from their bodies as the kiss deepened.

Kahron spread Bianca's legs above him as he reached between them to play in her moist folds. "Why it's so wet, huh?" he asked throatily.

"Why you so hard?" she countered, bending her head to capture one of his nipples into her mouth to nip lightly with her teeth.

He raised one hand to tangle in her curls, pressing her mouth closer to his nipple. Bianca suckled the nipple into her mouth hotly, following his lead.

For long, seemingly timeless moments, they caressed, fondled, and pleasured one another among their natural playground. Enjoying the warm feel of their bodies pressed together. Listening to the pounding beats of their hearts and the gasps of breath signaling be pleased. Legs and arms entwined as their bodies grinded and twisted together while they lips remained passionately locked. Their sighs and moans of pleasure blending with the sound of the summer breeze rustling the towering trees above and the cries of birds in flight.

As Bianca moved to straddle his thighs again, she leaned forward to press her breasts to his mouth, shivering when he suckled one and then the other in a rapid motion that was highly erotic. They hung in his face like beautiful chocolate pendulums and Kahron muzzled his face in between in that warm valley, enjoying the soft flesh lightly pressed against his face.

Bianca smiled lightly, wiggling her shoulders to make them jiggle lightly. "Shaking it like a salt shaker," she teased.

Kahron laughed and then twisted his face to capture one thick nipple in his mouth.

Bianca leaned up, his mouth making a slight "pluck" noise as she free her nipple from his mouth. Rising she lightly tapped her foot against the side of his strong buttocks, before turning to dash behind one of the massive tree trucks, the grass softer than cushion beneath her feet. Her thighs were slightly moist from her own juices and her swollen bud was numb from his bites, but she had never felt so aroused and alive with desire.

Kahron rose, quickly reaching for his wallet to pull out a condom. He massaged the solid length of his shaft as he tore the foil with his teeth and then sheathed himself, rolling the latex as far as it would reach.

Bianca peeked around the tree and saw Kahron advancing towards her, his covered penis leading him as it hung awkwardly and heavy from his muscled frame. Her eyes devoured every delicious inch, anxious for him to find her and have her. The muscle in his legs flexing as he moved. The tiny stream of sunlight glinting from his silver hair.

Kahron saw Bianca shift back behind the tree and he moved to hide behind a tree as well. *Two can play this game*. He walked further down behind the trees and then moved toward her from behind.

Bianca peeked behind the tree, surprised not to find him.

Kahron smiled at the sight of her shapely apple bottom tooted in the air as she leaned around the tree, obviously looking for him. He swiftly moved up to her and slid one strong arm around her waist. "Gotcha," he whispered thickly in her ear.

Bianca melted back against him even as her heart thundered in surprise. "Oh, you got me."

He released his hold to allow her body to slide down the length of his.

Bianca looked over her shoulder as she bent over at the waist and lightly wiggled her bottom against his heat as she outstretched her arms and placed her hands against the tree trunk.

Kahron looked down at the lips of her core open to him before he guided his shaft inside her slowly, inch by delicious inch, filling her snugly as her walls contracted against his length. He clenched his teeth at her tightness and her heat, his hands tightly squeezing her buttocks as he struggled for control.

Bianca winced slightly as she felt every bit of his thickness press against her walls and announce its presence. "Easy," she gasped, dropping her head between her arms.

Kahron's breathing was haggard. "Almost got all of it in, baby."

They both gasped hotly and shivered as he filled her completely, the soft hairs surrounding his shaft brushed lightly against her buttocks.

Kahron felt the excitement building in him as his member throbbed and he stilled his movement not wanting it to end before it even began. His hands moved up her velvet skin to grasp her hanging breasts tightly as he bent over and rested against her back.

Only as he felt his climax wane did he rise on his toes and began to pump his hips against her fleshy buttocks, bending his knees a bit to fit her better. His heated eyes locked on the sight of his tool sliding in and out of her with ease as her brown lips suctioned him. His mouth formed an O as Bianca began to grind back against him, causing her walls to release and then grasp his member tightly like a suction. "Easy, baby, easy," he moaned as he bit his bottom lip in pure satisfaction. "You gone make me come."

Bianca felt each of his strokes like a shot of pure electricity through her body. Each pump like a lifeline. She felt sexy and powerful as she arched her back and circled her hips like she wore a hoola-hoop that she couldn't let fall down. Each delicious thrust brought a moan of pleasure from deep within her. "Uhm," she sighed.

There was something primal and erotic about having wild sex in a remote but nonetheless publicly accessible forest. It seemed they were alone in the world—Adam and Eve—when in fact the highway was just beyond the trees as life continued and the cars whizzed by unaware that this man and his woman were sharing incredible sex with nature as an onlooker.

Excitement shimmied over their bodies as the air between them changed. Intensified. Deepened. Electrified.

The hum signaling the rise of their climax began to increase around them. The pace of their stroking increased. Their pumps were slick and hard like a well-oiled piston. Their heartbeats raced as they worked for their releases. Their bodies coated with a fine sheet of sweat.

As his body became hot and trembling as he got closer to coming, Kahron stood up straight and released a holler into the woods that bounced off the trees, the veins in his neck straining as each wave of euphoric pleasure washed over him. His thick penis jolted with spasm after spasm of his release filling her.

Bianca's fingers gripped the bark of the tree as she began to shudder. She squeezed her eyes shut, spiraling toward that place where sexual high reached its peak. "Harder," she begged Kahron with force.

Kahron pumped vigorously, reaching around her to press his fingers against the swollen bud between her legs as he did, knowing it would intensify her release.

"I'm coming," Bianca shouted, her body jerking as her poor heart galloped at a racehorse's pace.

She cried out hoarsely with each delicious wave.

They both shuddered as the waves subsided after long, delicious moments. Bianca stood straight with Kahron's rod still planted deeply within her and he held her tightly against him as she rose her arms to wrap around his neck.

"Damn," they sighed together.

Although Kahron felt weak and beat, he carried Bianca back to their pile of clothing, laying her down before he took the spot beside her. He pulled her body close to his. They lay there naked and exposed together still reveling in what they shared for a long time.

Bianca wanted to express how she felt to Kahron, but she didn't know how exactly to verbalize it. "Everything with you from the beginning has been so intense," she began as she lightly played with his fingers. "My attraction to you the first time I saw you on the back of the truck all the way up to what we just shared has been . . . so . . . powerful."

Kahron lightly kissed her sweaty brow. "I feel the same way, B."

"I'm not saying I'm in love, but I am saying that I care about you a lot and I have never felt this strongly about someone so quickly."

Kahron nodded as he looked down at their entwined fingers. "It just feels right," he added.

Bianca rolled over onto her stomach, propping her chin on her folded hands, as she looked out at the running stream. "I haven't made love with a man in nearly six years," she admitted softly.

Kahron pressed his hand onto the small of her back. "Are you regretting what happened?" he asked, his voice unsure.

Bianca turned her head and locked her eyes with his. "Never," she admitted fiercely.

He reached out to move a stray curl from her face. "I'm so glad I met you, B. I'm glad you came back to Holtsville. I'm glad that you just shared your body with me. I'm glad you're in my life."

Bianca smiled at him, softly and sweetly, leaning over to capture his lips with her own. "Ditto," she told him.

Kahron reached over and tweaked her nose.

10

To move or not to move: that is the question.

Bianca tapped the pen she was holding against her cheek as she lightly swiveled back and forth in the office chair. Her eyes shifted to the lease agreement on the desk before her. An agreement she had yet to sign.

The concept of moving back home was easy in theory, but there was a lot to be thought out. Pros and cons to be weighed. She thought the decision had been made until the realtor faxed the agreement to her and it was time to sign on the dotted line.

She reached across the desk for a notepad, drawing a line down the middle. She wrote *Pros* at the top of one side and *Cons* at the top of the other.

"Pros," she said lightly, before she began writing. When she was done she read the list aloud. "Nearer to Daddy. Rebuild the ranch. Possibly expanding business with second clinic. Extra cash flow from selling house in ATL. Kahron—'nuff said." She placed cartoonlike exclamation points next to his name.

Lord, she was sprung and that was no lie.

Her cheeks warmed as she remembered their tryst in the woods. "Uhm . . . uhm . . . uhm."

That man could work her like it was his J–O–B.

And work it he did . . . that night in the living room. The next day they snuck a quickie in this very office— her eyes shifted to the plush chaise lounge sitting before the fireplace. "If it could talk, the things it would tell," she said with a delighted little laugh.

Beyond the sex—the great, mind-blowing sex—they really enjoying spending time together. Be it lounging on the couch watching television—both were junkies of reality TV and blaxploitation films—or relaxing on his bed with his head in her lap as they read, or going horse-back riding over Kahron's property. They had slipped into a comfort zone with each other.

Bianca could hardly believe she had just been back in Holtsville for less than two weeks. Everything was moving so fast.

Her hazel-green eyes fell to the lease agreement and then to the notepad. The *Cons*. She read off each one as she wrote it: "Giving up clinic in Atlanta. Selling dream house. Possible disappointment in Daddy. Trishon."

She thought about it and then crossed off "giving up the clinic"—she could sell it and use the money to open a clinic here in Holtsville or neighboring Summerville, or she could acquire a loan against the business in Atlanta and open a second clinic in Holtsville and just expand her practice. Regardless, she was going to continue practicing veterinary medicine.

She crossed off "selling house." Her dream house, which she honestly loved and had decorated herself, had already increased considerably in value since she brought it. She could sell it and just build a replica or better in Holtsville.

"Disappointed by Daddy."

Her father was doing well in rehab. He called her and Trishon as often as he could. During each conversation he sounded stronger and more confident in his recovery.

Bianca had faith that he would be better, so she crossed that off the list as well.

Her feelings about Trishon she would just work on. If she moved she would be in her own home, with her own life, and if Trishon was what her father wanted—and she obviously was after fifteen years—then so be it.

There were other things to be considered. Things she hadn't written down. What of all her board and committee memberships? And Mimi? How would she make it without her diva friend strolling in with her quick wit and even quicker sip from her fancy little flask. Even Anton. He was a rogue, but he was also a good friend when she needed it.

Those were all excuses, though, and she knew it. She could resign the positions and just visit her friends back in Atlanta.

So, even with every Con dismissed, all excuses explained away, and a list of Pros she looked forward to, why was she still hesitant to sign the lease on the modern three-bedroom townhouse located in a gated community in Walterboro?

Dropping her pen atop the pad, she leaned back in the chair, letting it bounce back and forth slightly. She was still bouncing and her wrestling with her plans when Ralph knocked twice on the open office door.

Ralph was one of the two ranch hands she hired. He was tall and white with more freckles than anything. She knew it was childish, but when she looked at him she could just hear Eddie Murphy saying, "Opie Cunningham."

Bianca waved him in. "Come in, Ralph," she beckoned, grasping the desk's edge to pull her chair forward.

"Bad news, Ms. King," he said, removing his Stetson.

"What's up?"

"Looks like the new equipment's missing."

"What?" Bianca exclaimed, rising to her feet as her stomach lurched.

"Don and I we're going to start setting the supplies up in the new tack room, you know the way you said 'fore we left yesterday, and well . . ."

Bianca came around the desk. "What exactly is missing?"

"Everything, ma'am."

Bianca felt like she could throw up. She raced past Ralph to dash out the house, past her newly repaired vehicle, to eat up the distance between the house and the new barn with her feet.

Her lungs ached from the running and her heart raced from the exercise and fear. She barely stopped to pull open the door to the tack room. Her steps faltered and her eyes widened in disbelief.

She felt like her legs wanted to give out beneath her, but Bianca *refused* to fall.

All of it was gone.

All of it. Nearly $10,000 worth of supplies and equipment.

Bianca heard the door swing open behind her and she quickly composed herself with a cool face. *Never let 'em see you sweat, girl.*

She didn't know what was going on around here, but she was tired of sitting back and reacting to the crap somebody was pulling at that ranch. She was going to get to the bottom of it.

"I'll call the police," she told Ralph and Don, moving between their broad shoulders to leave the barn.

"Yes'm." Ralph said, his freckled face concerned.

"It's a damn shame," Don added.

Bianca said nothing else and just continued back up the worn path to the house. Her mind was too busy working. When had the thefts occurred? When the men left for the day it had been around 6 P.M. yesterday and everything had been where it belonged. An hour later she left to go to Kahron's and she'd gotten back around eleven and nothing had looked out of place. Then again, she hadn't exactly done a security sweep to ensure that. So the robbery had to take place while she was at Kahron's.

"I don't know which is worst."

Bianca looked up to find Trishon on the porch dressed entirely in red, a cigarette in hand. "I'm not in the mood for your gossip right now, Trishon, " she said, climbing the stairs of the porch.

"Umph, having one of your boyfriend's women puncture your tire or the same boyfriend who's trying to buy a business from underneath your father."

"Shut the hell up, Trishon," Bianca told her angrily, those tiger like eyes flashing their namesake. She was tired of holding her tongue and just a tad bit afraid that there was truth in her words.

"Ooh, so touchy, Bianca. I'm just trying to look out for you *and* my husband." Trishon released a stream of acrid smoke from her crimson lips that stained the butt. "I told you when you first got here that Kahron Strong was trouble with capital T, but did you listen? Hell to the no."

Bianca crossed her arms over her chest as she stepped closer to the woman. "It's funny that somebody who wants the town to forget their shady past can't muster enough humanity to do the same for someone else."

Trishon's eyes glittered. "You always thought you were better than me, Bianca King. You and your friends. You think I didn't hear ya'll laughing and whispering behind my back 'cause I ain't had fancy clothes and shoes like you."

"You're not the only one had it bad growing up, Trishon. When my mother died I ended up with a daddy who's a drunk and married to the town slut!" Bianca gasped a little and her eyes rounded as soon as she said the words.

Trishon's eyes cooled. "Sticks and stones, Bianca. Sticks and fucking stones."

Bianca closed her eyes, hating that she resorted to flinging childish insults at the woman. When she opened them again Trishon was climbing into her little red BMW and speeding off down the dirt road. "Damn," she whispered.

The anger she felt in that moment had nothing at all to do with her father's alcoholism or his marriage to Trishon. It had everything to do with her anger at Trishon striking out at Kahron and planting a seed of doubt that Kahron was playing her. In her mind there was always the hint of, "what if . . .".

Trishon stopped her car outside the battered and defeated trailer where she lived until she married Hank King. She could fit the whole pitiful 14 × 60 thing inside her home.

The grass and bush that surrounded the pale pink trailer was overgrown. One of the windows had cardboard taped on it. Their were sheets and towels at the window as makeshift curtains. The wooden steps were decrepit as if one good stomp could send it falling like dominoes.

The door opened suddenly and Trishon accelerated forward.

"Trishon! Trishon, come back, Trishon!"

She heard a woman's voice calling her name—probably her mother—but she kept on going determined to leave any aspect of that life—and those in it—behind.

Once they were done giving the police their statements, Bianca sent Ralph and Don home, telling them both they were off until Monday. She walked down to the barn, entering through the door to stand in the center of the massive structure.

"What made me think I could do this?" she asked herself in a soft voice, feeling defeated. As she walked in a slow circle around the barn her eyes took in all the empty stalls—stalls that needed to be filled.

She was tempted to call Kahron, but she didn't. Yes, it was nice to have someone to support you, but she didn't want to get in the habit of him being her first line of defense. She had opened her own prestigious practice, brought her own home, and lived a good life—all without a man dictating or leading her.

The "what ifs" were dogging her and Bianca needed to think some things through. Being caught up in Kahron might have just cost her ten grand, and that was a mistake she wasn't planning to make again.

Bianca strode out of the barn, her Reeboks making tiny puffs in the dirt as she did. She made sure to turn off the lights and securely lock up the barn with the newly installed padlocks—good use they were now.

She rushed back to the house and up the stairs, quickly throwing some items in a Louis Vuitton duffel. She scribbled a quick note to Trishon and taped it to her door, before jogging down the stairs and tossing the duffel and her purse into her trunk.

Bianca drove to Kahron's ranch, hoping he would understand. She turned down the road leading to the set back ranch, one hand playing in her nearly gone straw set curls while she steered with the other. She pulled up and parked in front of the house, leaving the car to climb the few steps onto the porch.

"How you doin'?"

Bianca turned on the top of the step to find one of Kahron's ranch hands sitting astride a horse at the foot of the steps. His keen, ebony eyes were on her. She smiled in greeting. "Hi . . ."

"Dante," he supplied, smiling at her and perusing her with those eyes in a way that quickly let Bianca know he was interested.

"Yes, Dante, that's right. How you doing?" she asked.

"Better now," he answered with a lick of lips that was such a bad imitation of LL Cool J.

He wasn't a bad looking man; in fact, he was boyishly handsome with a tall solid frame and a short afro that fit his face well. But, she thought him foolish to come on to her right in front of Kahron's house. Foolish or bold . . . maybe both.

"Kahron around?" she asked, wishing he didn't make her feel like she was naked and gyrating on a pole.

"Haven't seen him," he drawled.

Okay, you know what . . .

Bianca scratched her scalp and forced a smile. "How can you not see him and you're on his property?" she asked, trying to keep the censure from her voice.

Dante just shrugged slowly.

"You've been so helpful, Dante, thank you ever so much," she said, not bothering to hide the sarcasm as she turned and knocked on the door.

Maybe his housekeeper knew where he was.

"Anything I can help you with?" Dante asked from behind her. "I'm more than willing to . . . help you out."

He laughed low and cockily.

Bianca turned and put a hand on her hip as she tapped her finger against her lip, glanced down and then back up at him. "You know what, Dante, I have all the dick I need in my life right, so I won't be needing yours, but thanks for offering."

"You tell him, girlfriend."

Bianca turned and her jaw literally dropped at the sight of the beautiful woman standing before her in the doorway of her *man's* home. *Get it together, Bianca.*

"You must be Bianca. I recognize your from the photo on Mister Strong's nightstand," she said, her heavy accent prominent, her smile friendly.

The photo they took in his study with the digital camera. Bianca smiled in return, but that little piece of her that was as green as grass with envy wanted to tell the little señorita to hit the road.

"It's nice to meet you, Garcelle," Bianca said, deciding to take the high road of maturity and self-confidence. "Your cooking is delicious. I really loved the chicken and rice dish."

Garcelle leaned forward like an old friend and winked. "I will give you the recipe. Our little secret, no?"

Bianca didn't know if the woman was truly sincere or not, but she decided to trust her—with the stipulation that she would give her an old fashioned country girl whupping if she found out the woman was making a play for *her* Kahron.

"When I return," she told her. "Is Kahron around?"

"No, ma'am. He had to go to his father's ranch in Walterboro."

Bianca was disappointed. She wanted to taste his lips before she left. "I'll call him on his cell," she said. "Thanks, Garcelle."

"Your welcome."

Bianca turned as Garcelle walked back into the house. Dante was still sitting there, but Bianca decided to ignore him and his staring. She stepped down off the porch. He nudged his horse into her path. Bianca glared up at him and shifted to the left. He nudged the horse that way as well.

Bianca felt a bit of nervousness, but she showed none of it. Instead, she glared up at him. "Are you kidding me?" she snapped, incredulous.

"Sorry," he said finally, nudging the horse from in front of her.

Bianca glared at him as she moved to climb into her car. Even as she circled the car, she glanced in her rearview mirror and saw that he had turned to watch her retreat.

She ignored him, reaching for her cell phone to call Kahron's. It went to voice mail. Not bothering to leave a message, she flipped the phone close and dropped it onto the passenger seat.

As she sped away from the ranch she thought of Dante's intensity and it gave her chills.

Kahron turned his truck down the tree lined road leading to the King ranch. He headed straight from his parent's ranch in Walterboro to Bianca. They had dinner plans, but he didn't want to wait until then. He wanted to see her now.

He smiled as he passed the break in the trees that led to the spot where he made love to Bianca for the first time. His penis pumped to life between his thighs at the sultry memory and he could only shake his head as his smile grew.

Who knew that Bianca would be such a sexual wildcat?

And that she was. Her ardor matched his own and she gave herself to him freely without any restraints or inhibitions. When they united it was if they merged into one being and drifted in a world all their own where pleasure was king.

Oh yeah, she got me good and f'ed up. A fine shiver of desire raced through him as he thought of the way Bianca bit those juicy lips he loved when she was coming as he stroked deep within the sweetest walls ever.

Kahron neared the house and saw Papa Doc's brilliant red truck sitting next to Trishon's BMW, but Bianca's convertible was absent from its usual spot. *Maybe it's parked in the back.*

Kahron was just climbing out of his truck when Papa Doc walked out the front door. "What's up, Papa Doc?" Kahron asked friendly, as he jogged up the stairs.

Papa Doc held out his hand for Kahron to shake. "I was hoping to talk to Bianca, but Trishon just told me she's gone back to Atlanta."

Kahron frowned in confusion. He reached in his front pocket for his cell phone, forgetting that it needed to be charged up. "Yeah, I forgot she was headed back today," Kahron lied, not wanting to show his confusion.

Papa Doc leveled his coal black eyes on him. "I'll be heading on home then. Enjoy your night."

Kahron didn't bother trying to question Trishon—

the woman irked his nerves, and right now, as he struggled to fight the panic he felt that Bianca was gone for good, he wasn't in the mood to deal with Trishon's slick comments.

Kahron jogged down the stairs past Papa Doc, moving to get into his truck as Hershey barked at him from the rear of the truck. "See you later, Papa Doc," Kahron called out through the open window as he reversed the truck.

Papa Doc was patting his pockets. "Think I left my dang on lighter," he said, before turning to head back up the stairs. "'Night Kahron."

Kahron reversed in an arc and then accelerated forward down the lane. He was anxious to get home and call Bianca and find out just what was going on.

He had to admit to himself that he was afraid she was gone for good, even though that didn't make any since at all. Steering with one hand, he reached in his pocket for his cell phone and tried again to power it on. He flung it onto the passenger seat in frustration. It was useless to him and he didn't have his travel charger to get some juice flowing into it in the truck.

Accelerating fast enough to get a hefty ticket if the police stopped him, Kahron made it to his house in record time. Barely shutting off the truck he raced up the few stairs, quickly inserting his key to enter.

The scent of one of Garcelle's dishes filled the house, but he hardly noticed as he strode into the living room and snatched up his cordless. He scrolled through the caller ID. He felt flooded with relief at the sight of Bianca's cell phone number . . . initially.

Maybe she was calling to tell him it was over as she cruised back to her life in Atlanta.

Quickly he dialed her cell phone number, actually

pacing as it rang. His heart thudded against his chest like the constant slamming of a heavy wooden door.

One ring. Two. Three.

He thought she wasn't going to answer.

"Hey you," she said simply with that same soft tone that comforted him. As if she hadn't scared the devil out of him.

Kahron released a heavy breath and mouthed a quick, "Thank God," before he spoke. "Hey, you," he said in return, calm as ever.

"I've been trying to call you. I'm in Atlanta."

Yes, I know. "My phone's dead," he said, flopping down onto his sofa, dirty clothes and all, as he wiped his mouth with his lean and strong hands.

"Oh, okay so you didn't get my messages then."

"No." Kahron positioned his phone between his ear and shoulder as he pulled of his boots. "Was there an emergency at the clinic?"

"No."

The question of *why* hung in the void of their silence.

Bianca pulled her bare feet beneath her in the middle of her bed. She was home. Her domicile. Her haven. Still, she missed and craved Kahron as soon as she walked through the door. As his voice caressed the phone lines the craving increased to an intensity that left her breathless. "I can't think straight around you," she began, lightly biting the tip of her thumb nail. "I need to be able to think because I have some huge decisions to make."

She could count the seconds—or maybe even minutes—that Kahron remained silent.

"The robbery today wiped me out—"

"What robbery?"

"Someone stole all of the equipment and supplies I ordered for the ranch. All of it."

"Were you there when it happened?" he asked, concern evident in his voice.

Bianca shook her head, and then realized he couldn't see her. "No, it must have happened last night when I was at your place."

"You think I'm involved and that's why you went flying back to Atlanta?" he said, his voice cold.

"No, Kahron."

"Then why did you leave? When are you coming back? Hell . . . *are* you coming back?"

"It's just for the weekend, Kahron, and I'm sorry I didn't tell you before I left." She turned her troubled eyes to the open balcony doors. "A lot had happened in the last two weeks and straight up, I just needed to step away from it all for a minute and regroup."

"Even me?"

"Yes, even you," she admitted

"I want you to run to me, not from me, B."

"For so long it's just been me, myself, and I, you know?"

"I told you by the stream that we weren't ready for sex," he reminded her.

Bianca rolled out of bed, the phone clutched to her ear. "It's not the sex."

"Then what is it?"

"It's my heart," she whispered, moving to stand on the balcony. "Trusting a man with your heart is way deeper than trusting him with your body."

"You can trust me with all of you, B."

Bianca felt warmed by his words and for a few precious moments she let herself be surrounded and comforted by them. "I would have to trust you with Garcelle the gorgeous roaming around your house all day," she told, lightening the mood.

"Oh, you met Garcelle, huh?" he asked, his voice hesitant.

Bianca stuck her tongue in her cheek. "Oh, yes."

"She's a really sweet girl."

"Just make sure you don't *taste* how sweet she is. You feel me, cowboy?"

Kahron laughter filled the line, rich and full. "B, you crazy. I have all the woman I need in you."

Bianca let her hand trail down the deep vee of her nightgown. "Oh trust, I'm very secure in my abilities to satisfy you. That's *my* dick and I know it is," she boasted, shifting her hands to lightly tease her own nipples as they tightened into chocolate buds. "I try to drain it."

Kahron laughed huskily into the phone. "And that's my stuff, right?"

"Yup." Bianca pressed her back against the door frame as she rubbed her hand down her leg, her fingers searching and finding the slick folds of her core. "I'm playing in your stuff right now."

"Damn," Kahron swore softly.

Bianca drew air between her teeth as she drew light circles around the pulsing rose colored bud. Her lower body jerked a little from the pressure she put on the sensitive flesh and she moaned lightly.

"If I pack now and hit the road I an be in ATL by midnight, B," he told her in the deepest voice she ever heard emitted from him.

Bianca thought of his fingers replacing her own. Damn, why couldn't she resist this man? "Come on," she told him.

11

Bianca left the comfort of Kahron's arms as he slept, reaching to the floor for her bathrobe to cover her naked frame. She moved to his side of the bed and pulled the sheet up to his waist, but not without a leisurely perusal of every bit of his chiseled frame—including his penis, which was thick and impressive even at rest as it lay curled against his navel.

They had made love from the moment he entered her home. With fierceness on the floor of the foyer. With tenderness on the balcony of her bedroom. Almost frantically in the shower. Playfully in the kitchen with the coolness of the refrigerator against her back and buttocks.

All night. Over and over until finally at dawn Bianca gave one final spin of her hips to send them both spiraling into ecstasy.

That had been just a few precious hours ago and even though her body was drained, Bianca decided to make breakfast for her man. Her man. That sounded so good.

Casting him one final glance as he snored lightly with his mouth ajar, Bianca left her bedroom suite. She descended the stairs, walking to the left of the staircase to enter her kitchen. The first thing she did was start a pot of coffee. She needed her "kick ass" iced coffee to replace the energy they depleted last night.

With Kahron's presence in her home, Bianca's plans of getting her mind straight without him was gone to pot. It felt good to have him here on her turf, but decisions still had to be made.

Bianca was chopping ingredients to go into the shredded potatoes she was frying. Ham. Green peppers. Onions. Cheese. Huddle House style.

She was singing Etta James' "At Last" as she stirred eggs in a copper bowl when she noticed Mimi walking up the drive, dressed to the nines in a lemon suit with a matching clutch purse like she had somewhere to be— Bianca knew better.

Glad to see her quirky friend, Bianca met her at the door, pulling it open wide. "Well, good morning, Ms. Mimi."

Mimi kissed the air next to each of Bianca's cheeks. "Hairdresser on strike, sweetie?" was the first thing out of Mimi's mouth.

"Missed you too," Bianca drawled dryly, closing the door as Mimi strolled into the kitchen like *she* paid the mortgage.

"If I didn't know any better I would say you had a sweat out, boo."

Bianca said nothing, moving to pour the eggs into the warmed frying pan.

Mimi froze. She took in Bianca's mussed hair and the slinky and sexy robe, to the large breakfast she was preparing. Her face transformed as she smiled. "Somebody's been naughty," she said in a little sing-song fashion.

Bianca dropped her head and bit her bottom lip to keep from smiling.

"Oooh, somebody's been very, huh, what . . . naughty,

that's right, sweetie. *Nasty* even," she teased, sitting her purse on the island as she eyed Bianca.

With Bianca's light complexion her blushing was clear.

Mimi moved over to the entrance of the kitchen, her eyes devilish. "And may I presume this is your little cowboy you told me about that knocked your feet, huh?"

"Don't you mean boots, Mimi?"

"Boots, feet, ass . . . whatever it was I'm sure they were pointed at the ceiling, sweetie."

Bianca finished scrambling her eggs and turned the fire off from under the hash browns. When she turned from the stove, Mimi was gone. Bianca frowned and then her eyes rounded. She took off out the kitchen, nearly slipping on the tiled floor as she turned the corner to enter the foyer and dash up the stairs two at a time.

She rolled her eyes at her bedroom door opened wide.

"So you're Kahron. Well, I just love that silver hair on you," she heard Mimi say.

"Yes, ma'am. Thank you, ma'am," Kahron answered.

She entered to find Mimi sitting on the edge of the bed and Kahron looking like a deer caught in headlights as he held the sheet up to his chin. He leaned to the right a little to give Bianca a meaningful stare that said, "Help."

"So are there any older versions of you back in HunkyTonk?" she asked in that nasal voice with a smile that was purely delighted as she winked at him and wiggled her shoulders comically.

"That's enough, Oprah Winfrey," Bianca said, moving to guide Mimi off the bed.

"You know you remind me of my husband," Mimi said over her shoulder as Bianca steered her to the door. "Now was it Darwin, James, or Pedro. No, no . . . it was definitely, Gary . . . I think."

Bianca glanced over her shoulder. Kahron was shaking his head and smiling. "Breakfast is ready," she told him.

"No, I'm positive it was Ricky."

Bianca closed the door behind them.

Once he was sure Mimi wouldn't burst back through the door, Kahron flung the sheet back and rose from the bed nude. His member hung lifelessly between his legs, nearly drained from his night with Bianca, swinging between his thighs like third arm as he made his way to her adjoining bath to relieve himself.

Kahron was impressed by Bianca's home. It was beautiful and stylish but comfortable—it suited her perfectly. He planned to ask her to take her by the clinic. It was a huge part of her life and he wanted to see that as well. He would use this weekend to explore and learn more about this woman who was fast becoming an integral part of his life.

He moved back into the bedroom to retrieve his leather duffel bag from by the door. He retrieved his monogrammed grooming bag and his cell phone. As he walked into the bathroom, he dialed his brother Kade's cell phone.

"Kade Strong."

"Hey, man, this Kahron. I need a favor." Kahron set his bag on the pedestal sink.

"Name it."

"I'm in Atlanta for the weekend—"

"Well damn, when you leave?"

Kahron leaned in to peer at his reflection in the ornate mirror over the sink. He wondered if he should shave. "About eight last night."

"You shoulda told me you were headed to ATL I woulda rode with you."

"Uh . . . no."

"Oh. You with Bianca?"

"Uh . . . yeah."

"What she say about the break-in?"

"Damn word travels fast." Kahron reached into his bag for his toothbrush.

"That's Holtsville for you. How's she doing?"

"She's pissed, and rightly so," Kahron said. "She's taken some tough knocks with her Dad, the car, and now the break-in. That's why she needed a break and came home."

"Maybe she'll give up on Holtsville all together. With Hank back in charge it won't be long before he f's up again and has to sell the land."

"Yeah, tell me about it." Kahron turned on the faucet, running warm water over the bristles of his toothbrush before putting toothpaste on it.

"I just know King will sell that land to you one of these days."

Kahron thought about that for a moment. "Bianca really wants her father's business to survive. It's important to her."

"So what you saying, you don't want the land now?"

"Not if it means hoping and wishing Bianca fails. Hell no." Kahron leaned down to brush the reside from his teeth, mouth, and tongue.

"Good. Now what's the favor?"

Kahron rinsed his mouth. "Just keep an eye on my ranch for me."

"Got you covered, little bro."

Kahron grabbed a washcloth from Bianca's bathroom closet. "No worries 'bout that. I'll holla at you when I get back."

He quickly washed his face and then his privates at the sink. Feeling somewhat refreshed he strode out of the bathroom and grabbed plaid pajama pants and a black tank from his bag. Soon he was jogging down the stairs, the scent of Bianca's breakfast leading him all the way.

"Sweetie, you really like him, don't you?"

Kahron paused on the steps at Mimi's question.

"Yes. Yes, I do. I really . . . really do."

Kahron's smile broadened and he continued down.

"But?"

He paused again.

"But nothing, Mimi."

"Lie to me, but sweetie, but don't lie to yourself, say what say who."

Kahron continued down the stairs and entered the kitchen before he could overhear any more. Anything Bianca had to say about him he wanted her to say to him directly and not eavesdrop on it like a punk. "Breakfast smells good," he said, wanting to announce his presence.

Bianca set a plate on a clear placemat at the end of the island. "Here you go, baby."

Kahron sat down before the plate, but his mind was heavy on just what doubts Mimi saw in Bianca about their relationship. Of course, he thought of her initial accusation that he was trying to run her father out of business. *Does she think I stole her equipment?*

Bianca sat down with her own plate as Mimi and she discussed some of the gossip of their subdivision. At one point she reached over and caressed his hand, smiling over at him like he was the bread for her butter. The rainbow after her rain.

That was all well and good, but what kind of relationship did they have if she didn't trust him . . . and trust was important to him. He thought of all the drama with

Shauna: finding her driving to his house at three in the morning just to make sure he was home like he said; her overreacting to finding him talking to a woman at his family cookout—a woman that she didn't bother to let him explain was his cousin. So many stupid incidents that made them the talk of Holtsville.

Kahron shifted his eyes to Bianca.

Would trust be the end of them as well?

"Dinner party tonight at my house," Mimi announced, taking a dainty sip of her tomato juice as her food remained untouched. "I'm gone introduce my new favorite couple to Atlanta."

Bianca eyed that glass knowing somewhere along the line Mimi had spiked the drink. What appeared to be an innocent glass of tomato juice was in fact her own little Bloody Mary. The woman was a sponge. Who else could soak up the amount of liquor she did and not show one hint of its effect? Should she demand from her friend the same sobriety she demanded for her father? Was she a hypocrite?

"Mimi, you don't have to do that," Bianca said, shifting her eyes to Kahron. She let them rest there momentarily when she noticed the pensive look on his face as he pushed his food around on his plate with his fork.

"Too late, sweetie. It's a done deal," Mimi said. "Besides my cook needs something to do and a little last minute soiree is just the thing to snap her back to attention."

Bianca knew it was useless to debate the matter further. Dinner at Mimi's it is. "Something wrong, baby?" she asked, reaching over to massage Kahron's arm.

Kahron leaned forward and covered her hand with

his own . . . warmly, securely. "I'm fine . . . just tired that's all."

Mimi took a sip of her drink and went, "Humph, I bet, sweetie."

Bianca bit her bottom lip, her eyes bright as she turned and presented her shoulder to Kahron. "Come on. Give me my due. You know how we do," she told him, as she looked over her shoulder at him.

Kahron lifted his hand to pat her on the back twice, pretending to act begrudgingly.

It was a little game they played. After sex, if one had truly excelled over the other at pleasing each other, then a pat on the back was given.

Bianca laughed triumphantly and did the cabbage patch.

"Ah, my husbands and I were like that once," Mimi sighed in pleasure.

Bianca and Kahron shared an amused look.

With one hand Mimi reached across the island for one of Kahron's strong hands and reached across with the other for Bianca's. "Love is, huh, what . . . wonderful, that's right, Sweeties. That's right."

Bianca and Kahron shared a long look.

Love? Do I love Kahron? I want him. Desire him. Lust him. Enjoy him. Crave him. And at times, I need him. But do I love him?

Mimi rose. "I got a lot to do."

"Don't strain too much ordering the cook around, *dah*-ling," Bianca teased.

Mimi pushed her purse under her arm. "Good help is so hard to find," she said with the utmost seriousness.

The watched as Mimi strutted to the door. She turned suddenly, walked back to the island, and drained her glass with a tilt of her head. Without another word she turned and strode out the door.

"She's . . . different," Kahron said.

"Definitely." Bianca moved to stand behind Kahron and massage his shoulders.

"So I get to meet all your friends tonight, huh?"

"Definitely." She slipped her hands down under his shirt to tease his nipples to hardness with ease.

"Will you show me your clinic today?"

"Definitely." She withdrew her hands to wrap them around his waist and slide them in his pants to gather his limp chocolate penis into one hand snugly.

"And I want you to show me your Atlanta?"

"Definitely." She stroked him slowly to hardness, her lips lightly grazing his nape.

Kahron let his head fall back on her shoulder. "But first were gonna see who gets the pat on the back," he groaned in drawn out pleasure.

"*Definitely*."

Trishon stretched her limbs like she was making snow angels in the middle of the bed. It felt good to have it to herself. After having to sleep with three sisters nearly all her life, she relished having such a big and comfortable bed all to herself. In truth she suggested to Hank ages ago that they sleep in separate rooms, but he was having none of that. Didn't matter. Most times he stumbled in drunk and she left him where he dropped: on the floor in the foyer, on the stairs, in the bathroom. It didn't matter.

She rose from the bed naked and left the room, enjoying the freedom of being in this house—*her* house— all alone.

Naked and feeling free, she wandered throughout the entire house. Each room. Both upstairs and down. She was counting her blessings. Every piece of furniture. The abundance of food in the refrigerator and pantry. All of her clothes. Shoes. Perfume bottles. Even down to the washcloths and towels. Everything she touched lightly with a smile.

Now Hank was getting sober. She had to admit to a bit of fear. Every year of their marriage she had been married to this man under the influence of alcohol. Would sobriety change him? Would their marriage be the same?

No doubt her free reign over his money would end. Bianca was already watching every penny until Trishon had yet to shop in two weeks unless it was for necessities.

Life was changing, and she had to wonder what other changes were in store.

"Are you sure this is what you want to do, Bianca?"

Bianca looked from Dr. Harry Henley and Dr. Susan Levine, the two vets she hired on to assist with her practice. Her eyes rested back on Harry, the one who asked the question. "Yes, and I wanted to discuss it with you and see how you both felt about my decision to move to Holtsville? I'm thinking of selling the practice and I wanted to know if I did would either—or both of you— be interested?"

"Bianca, isn't this a little sudden?" Susan asked, her face round mocha face concerned.

Bianca rose from the chair in front of Harry's desk and paced a bit. "Yes, and I'm still feeling my way through everything, but I'm ninety percent sure this is what I want to do."

"When will you be one hundred percent sure?" Harry

asked, his reddish spectacles contrasting with his pale complexion.

"I should make a firm decision in about thirty days. I'm going to hire someone to appraise the value of the business, check out its worth. I still need to tie up some loose ends in Holtsville, and then there's my house—"

"So you would be selling your home here in Atlanta as well?" Susan asked.

Bianca crossed her arms over her chest and looked down at her colleague, seeing her clear interest. "With a move back to Holtsville? Definitely."

Susan just nodded and stroked her chin with her slender fingers.

"I guess right now what I am asking for is some time," Bianca began. "For now I need at least another month in Holtsville and if you guys could pick up my slack around here I would appreciate it."

"No problem, Bianca."

"Got you covered."

Bianca smiled warmly at them both. "Thanks. I really appreciate it. I'll come back and forth during the month, of course, so I won't be dropping off the face of the earth all together."

Harry and Susan shared a look and Bianca knew they were seriously considering ownership of the practice. It was a viable and thriving business—she made sure of that. The transition would be very easy for either—or both—because they were already practicing at the clinic.

"I'm gonna go to my office and catch up on some things." Bianca walked to the door. "You both know how to reach me."

She walked out and headed down the corridor to her large office at the rear of the building. She found Kahron sitting behind her desk playing solitaire on her flat screen computer. "Hey you," she said, closing the door behind her.

Kahron looked up as Bianca came to stand beside him and go through the stack of mail on her desk. "You're beautiful, B," he said.

She bumped his shoulder with her hip. "Thank you. You ain't so bad yourself."

"And you know what else?" he asked.

"What?"

"I'm proud of you."

Bianca looked down at him as he turned in the chair to face her, leaning back as he looked up at her. "For?" she asked, touched by the compliment.

"All of those awards at your house and this practice. I mean you did all of that by yourself and I, I mean, I'm really proud of you."

She saw the truth in his eyes and moved to sit down on his lap, her arms snaking around his neck. "Thank you," she told him, with a brief press of her lips to his own.

Kahron hand rested comfortable on her hip. "This facility is awesome and Holtsville can use something just like this. I mean, Holtsville is . . . getting something just like this, right?"

Bianca rubbed her hand against his silver shadow of a beard. "Is this your way of asking If I've changed my mind about moving back to Holtsville?"

Kahron slid his hand into her back pocket and let it rest against the warmth of her bottom. "That house, this practice, your life here. It's a lot to give up, B."

"Yes, yes it is," she admitted.

Kahron raised his hand from her pocket to lightly rub circles into her lower back. "If you do half as good with your father's ranch as you did with this clinic, I know everything will work out."

Bianca outlined his lips with her finger. "So I'm not setting myself up for the biggest disappointment of my life?"

Kahron shrugged lightly. "Not when it comes to me, B. Anything else I can't guarantee."

Bianca met his eyes, searching.

"This right here. You and me. This is good to go. Trust me."

She smiled as he kissed her fingertips.

12

Hours later, Bianca and Kahron rushed back to her house to get ready for Mimi's impromptu dinner party. After a greasy and oh so good lunch of ribs and baked beans at Fat Matt's Rib Shack on Piedmont, the couple did it up around Atlanta in true tourist fashion. They respected the history and the magnificence of The King Center on Auburn Avenue, and then headed to Auburn Street, where they strolled and enjoyed the many African-American–owned businesses on the street known as "Sweet Auburn." When they returned to Bianca's parked car they had bags filled with books, jewelry, and clothing. Last, at Kahron's request, Bianca took him to the Centennial Olympic Park, where children enjoyed running through the dancing fountains shaped like the Olympic symbol of five rings.

Bianca saw parts of Atlanta in one day that she never sought out during all the years she called the city home. She was glad she shared that view of Atlanta with Kahron.

They discovered even more about each other. Both were knowledgeable on black history and black consciousness, enjoying the writings of Cornel West, Henry

Louis Gates, Jr., and Michael Dyson. Kahron was more of a clothes horse, whereas Bianca craved jewelry. He wanted five kids or more; Bianca thought two—one boy and one girl—was better. They both were generous, gladly giving offerings to less-fortunate souls who panhandled at the park.

They had broken through to some of the many layers that made them unique, yet both knew they were many more layers to discover, and that came with time and commitment—something to which both were open.

"B, what should I wear?" Kahron hollered to her in the bathroom.

Bianca walked to the open bathroom door, her arms behind her back as she undid her bra. "Dressy casual," she told him.

"Isn't that like saying 'dry wet' or 'cool heat', B?"

"Ha, ha, ha."

Kahron glanced up and caught a swift glimpse of Bianca's smooth bottom and endless legs as she finished undressing. He dropped the striped shirt he held and moved across the room to lean in the doorway to watch his woman as she turned on the shower.

Bianca stood beneath the showerhead hanging from the ceiling, letting the water plaster her loosely curled hair to her head before flowing like waterfalls down every inch of her body. She reached for a bottle and quickly shampooed the rest of the straw set curls from her hair.

Kahron felt that familiar stirring as suds drizzled down her shoulders to coat her breasts until just the hard tips of her nipples peaked through the white foam.

Bianca rinsed the rest of the suds from her hair and then her body. She reached for a bar of soap, rubbing it in circles across her body. Each full breast. Arms. Stomach.

She bent to do her legs—left and then right. She rose to slide the bar between her legs.

That's when her eyes locked on Kahron.

Nothing was more erotic to him than that moment as Bianca stood there, naked, wet, and sleek as the steam swirled around her like a shifting fog. He knew that image would stay locked in his memory for a long time.

He stripped off his clothes in record time.

The shower door opened and the steam escaped to surround his sculptured bronze nakedness as he stepped inside to pull Bianca's body against his with a moan of pleasure. Their lips locked hungrily as water poured down upon them. The steam caressed their back, buttocks, and legs like a third member of ménage á trois.

They caressed each other, the water making their hands glide over each other's bodies with ease as their heads moved from left to right with each kiss. They inhaled deeply of the refreshing steam as it thickened.

Kahron took the soap from Bianca and began to lather her body. Dropping the soap, he turned her and drew her back to him so that his erection settled upward between her buttocks, cupped like a hot dog in buns. As he let his hands glide down to squeeze her breasts and lightly tweak her chocolate nipples, he lifted up on his toes to pump his hips. His penis glided up and down between her buttocks, the soap suds made the movement sleek and intensified.

Bianca shifted her hand down to press her middle finger to the swollen bud between her legs. She gasped at the feel of her own touch as she began to shake her finger across the sensitive flesh.

Kahron tilted his head to the left and leaned back to look at the motion of his penis as he moved his hands down to grasp Bianca's buttocks tightly. That tightened the friction of her flesh against his flesh and his mouth formed into an O as he kept pumping until he felt his thighs quivering with the rise of his climax.

Bianca began to shiver and she increased the light friction against her bud as she felt that spiral of pleasure. One of his hands rose to cup her breast tightly, his thick thumb and forefinger rolling her nipple—she cried out hoarsely and flung her head back. The water filled her mouth.

Kahron's grip on her buttocks deepened and the water sprung from their bodies from the furious contact. He bit his bottom lip as his brows furrowed, working furiously for the nut. The cords in his neck strained as the first climatic squirts of his release coated Bianca's back and buttocks and his stomach just before the water washed it away.

"Whew," Bianca sighed as she turned to grasp Kahron's penis and squeeze the last of his release from his member.

"Do we have to go to Mimi's?" Kahron asked, as he reached for another bar of soap and a washcloth.

Bianca released Kahron now limp member. Raising her arm playfully she let him wash her. "Yup."

"What about your hair?" he asked, as he rubbed the rag in circles over her back and buttocks.

"My straw set was too through, so I'm going to blow dry it and bump the ends."

She winked as he even lifted one leg to clean her intimacy thoroughly. She loved their comfortable nature with each other.

"Okay, all done," he told her.

Bianca stepped around him and opened the shower door.

"Hey," he called out. "My turn."

"Next time," she told him with a laugh.

Kahron used the wet rag to lightly tap her buttocks.

She flipped him the bird before closing the shower door behind her. "And hurry up, Kahron, we don't have all day," she called to him teasingly.

Kahron just shook his head and finished his shower. He truly felt like climbing into bed and sleeping until his body recouped from all the day's activities—in and out the shower.

He turned off the shower and stepped out, wrapping his towel around his waist as he did. Bianca was standing nude before the sink as she finished blow drying her hair. He moved to stand at the other sink to brush his teeth as he allowed the majority of his body to air dry.

Kahron brushed his teeth, but his eyes were on Bianca's reflection as she raked her fingers through her hair. Auburn locks that was now straight and thick, flowing to her shoulders.

He never thought she looked more beautiful. Her face was free of its usual light make-up, and her features were more prominent without the hair to distract from it. She caught his eye in the mirror and smiled at him.

Damn, I love her.

The phone rang.

"I bet that's Mimi," Bianca said before leaving the bathroom.

Kahron looked at his own reflection. His face was slightly surprised at his own thoughts. He loved Bianca?

No, man, not yet. Kahron bent down to rinse his mouth, rising to stare at his reflection again. *Right?*

Bianca strolled back into the bathroom. "Mimi said move it or lose it, pretty boy. Oh, and that is a quote."

He turned to stare down at her. *Do I love you?* It was to soon. He thought he knew Shauna, but what he knew and what he thought he loved had been an image. The real Shauna—the insecure, jealous, and vindictive one—didn't show her true colors until later.

Love?

They met in their usual place, a deserted and decrepit barn in the middle of a dense, overgrown area. The floors were nothing more than dirt. Field mice and spiders called it home.

But it was *their* place.

Atop that lone air mattress on the floor he let his woman, his Kitten, take his hardness into her mouth until the coarse hairs of his crotch touched her lips. She was just teasing the tip with her tongue when his cell phone rang.

"Damn," he swore, not wanting to answer it, but knowing that he had to.

He reached over onto the dirty floor for his cell phone, his Kitten followed right along with his slightly shifting hips, his erection planted deeply within her throat.

"Yeah."

"You alone?"

"Yeah," he lied.

"And you know what to do with the stuff?"

His eyes shifted to the boxes in the corner. "Yup," he said, his teeth clenching as her lips suctioned him harder.

"Call and let me know when it's done."

"Yeah."

He dropped the phone once the call ended and let out a holler that floated to the worn roof as his body jerked with each spasmodic release of his seed.

* * *

Armand stood in the corner of Mimi's dining room, his eyes locked on Bianca and Kahron. He hated the jealousy that he felt. He honestly had wanted Bianca for himself, but she never took him seriously. Never seemed interested in welcoming a man into her life. At least that's what he thought.

"She's really happy, isn't she, Armando?"

He looked down at Mimi's petite figure standing beside him in a crimson pantsuit. He just shrugged, not bothering to remind her for the umpteenth time that his name was *Armand*.

"You know I always thought you were a good friend to our little Bianca, Sweetie, when you weren't trying to French talk her into bed."

Armand remained silent, frowning as Kahron pulled Bianca to him for a quick hug.

"And I know you have enough class to be happy for a friend and not sulk in a corner like a, huh, what . . . spoiled Frenchman, that's right, Sweetie."

Armand looked down at Mimi, a woman he never took seriously.

"And I know I wouldn't want a party full of people knowing that my friend finding happiness bothered me so much, but hey, everybody's different, Frenchie."

"Point made, Mimi."

"Good."

Bianca was standing on the balcony leading from Mimi's elaborately decorated ballroom, her flute of sparkling cider nearly forgotten as she took that moment to think through her life.

The Atlanta landscape was beautiful, but it wasn't home. It never really had been home. Her father wasn't here. The ranch where she grew up and nourished her love of horses wasn't here. Kahron wasn't here . . . usually.

And the robbery, the vandalism on her car, someone trying to run her father out of business—it all brought out that don't "f" with me attitude. She wanted to stand and prove to them that Kings didn't scare easily. She wanted to meet the challenge and bring the ranch back to what it used to be. She wanted to go home and stop running.

Sighing, she took a deep sip of her cider, wishing for a minute that is was something stronger. She never had been a drinker before, and with her father in rehab, Bianca made the choice to stop drinking all together. Her silent support of his struggles with alcohol.

"*Je vous manquerai, beau.*"

Bianca turned just as Armand strolled out onto the balcony.

"You know what, Armand, I can honestly say I'll miss you, too," she told him, reaching to lightly touch his hand where it sat on the wrought iron rail.

"So you're really moving, huh?"

Bianca thought about it and nodded. "Yes. Yes, I am," she said, as if answering her own question as well.

"Just call me if you need anything. Anything at all, *mon amour.*"

"I might take you up on that," she joked.

They fell silent, both nursing their drink and absorbing the beauty of the summer night in Georgia.

"*Je vous aime, Bianca. Je toujours vous ai aimé.*"

Bianca looked up to find Armand's piercing eyes looking down on her. "No, Armand. You do not love me. You have never loved me. You love the chase. Every woman from here to the moon loves that face and that accent. They throw themselves at you, while I offered you something you hadn't received in along time . . . a challenge."

He started to speak but she shook her head. "You don't love me and you know it, Casanova. You just hate that another man got your prize, you big spoiled baby."

He smiled. "Okay, you're right. I'm not *in* love with you."

Bianca nodded in satisfaction.

"But I do love you and I wish you the best, Bianca."

"Now *that* I'll accept," she told him, allowing him to pull her into his arms for a quick hug.

"I had fun tonight."

Bianca left the bathroom rubbing moisturizer on her face as she smiled at Kahron's words. "Good," she told him, as she kicked off her slippers, turned off the lone lit lamp, and crawled into bed beside him. "Mimi's going to come to Holtsville for the big grand opening of the ranch."

Kahron turned on his side and pulled Bianca's body back against his with one strong arm. He enjoyed the feel of her satin pajamas against him. "I can't picture Mimi on a ranch," he mused, lightly kissing her neck before he settled his head back onto his pillow. "It's good that she wants to come support you."

Bianca snorted. "Mimi's reasons for coming to the ranch are not *that* honorable, trust me."

"Well, what's the reason?" he asked, his hand resting comfortably against her belly.

"Oh, no, I'm not saying."

"Why?"

"Because you gonna thinks she's . . . odd."

"Too late for that."

Bianca nudged him with her elbow.

"Come on, she is . . . *different*."

"She's unique and I love her to death, Kahron."

"Why does she really want to come to the ranch?"

Bianca rolled her eyes heavenward and looked over her shoulder at him, as if she could really see his face in the darkness. "You're like a dog on a bone."

"More like a dog with a bone," he told her, pressing his penis into her rear.

Bianca laughed. "Uh, more like a dog in search of a bone," she joked, because he wasn't hard and erect.

He pinched her bottom and Bianca squealed.

"Come on, tell me," he insisted.

"If I hear this again I'll kill you and bury you and then burn the spot where I buried you," she warned him.

Kahron remained silent.

"She wants to see how we collect semen from the horses."

"Eew."

"Kill, bury, burn."

"Gotcha."

They both laughed a little.

"You know I like to sleep with the TV on."

Bianca groaned. "Aw, hell to the no. I like it quiet. I'm a light sleeper."

"I had the TV on last night."

"We didn't do much sleeping last night," she reminded him in the darkness.

Kahron hands rose to squeeze her breast lightly, his fingers lightly grazing her nipple.

Bianca placed her hand atop his. "I am too tired for one of your Kahron specials, baby."

"Thank God," he said with obvious relief, his hand

drifting back down to rest comfortably on her hip. "I'm beat my damn self. I'll just have to try it your way."

"Thanks," Bianca said, her voice already thickening with sleep.

Moments later her snores filled the quiet and Kahron found it was just enough noise to lull him to sleep.

Kade was in Holtsville that Sunday morning for a whist tournament at Charlie's. He came down early to run by Kahron's first.

He pulled his Ford Expedition in front of the house when the front door opened. He started to reach for his hunting pistol in the glove compartment, but his hand paused when he saw a woman step out onto the porch.

She looked up toward him in surprise.

He stepped out of his truck and moved toward her. "What are you doing in there?" he asked, his voice hard.

A face that had been slightly confused flashed with anger. "My job. What are you doing 'round here, besides being rude?" she asked, her Spanish accent prominent.

Her coloring was so deeply bronzed that he was initially surprised at her accent. "Are *you* Garcelle?" he asked, tilting his head back to look up at where she stood on the top step of the porch. She was a looker, there was no doubt about that, and the flash of eyes showed her spunk.

"Why does everybody say that when they meet me?" she asked. "*Si*, I am Garcelle."

Kade eyes took in the way her white T-shirt hugged her small, plum-sized breasts and her dark denim skirt hung low on her wide hips falling just below her knee to show the shapely contours of her calves. Her hair flowed over her shoulders and her hands were on hips that were made to be held. Somehow, she was able to look sexy and innocent all at once.

Kade felt guilt at the strong desire he felt for her.

"Are you related to Mister Strong?" she asked, flipping her hair over her shoulder.

"Are you supposed to be here today?"

"Why else would I be here?"

"That's what I want to know."

"Are you kidding me?"

Kade reached for his cell phone and dialed Kahron's cell number.

Garcelle mumbled something in Spanish and then turned and walked back into the house.

Kade took the stairs two at a time only to find the door was locked. He started searching for his spare key. Remembering it was on his key ring, he jogged back down the stairs to his SUV.

His phone dropped and closed, but as soon as he stooped to pick it up it began to ring. "Yeah."

"Man, why are you scaring my housekeeper?"

Kade frowned at the sound of Kahron's voice. "She called you?"

"Yes, saying some silver haired lunatic was outside accusing her of stealing or something?"

Kade's frowned deepened.

"Do you know how many housekeepers I've had?"

"Yeah."

"Do you know how many horror stories I could recite about each one?"

"Yeah, but . . ."

"But hell," Kahron stressed jokingly. "I need a new housekeeper like I need a hole in the head."

Kade dropped his head and laughed, the tension

easing from his broad shoulders. "I guess I did over react. She caught me off guard."

"Trust me. My first sight of her caught me off guard, too."

"Where's Bianca?"

"In her car ahead of me. We're on our way back."

"Think you'll make it for the whist tournament."

"I should."

"Cool. See you then."

Kade flipped his phone closed and made his way back up the stairs. He knocked twice and the door immediately opened. Her presence filled the doorway and Kade was again taken aback by the all of her—and for him that spelled trouble.

"With as much racism and prejudice blacks have faced in the country I don't understand why you all think so badly of Hispanics. I am not a thief. I do not know any thieves. Everyone I know works hard . . . just like me."

"I'm sorry, Garcelle. I wasn't trying to imply you were steal . . ."

Her raised brow stopped his words.

"It had nothing to do with you being Hispanic," he insisted with honesty.

"*Ridículo*," she muttered.

"Did you just call me ridiculous?"

"If the shoe fits." Garcelle shrugged.

"Look I apologize again for jumping to conclusions, okay," he grounded at her, before turning and jumping into his Expedition. He steered the truck down the path leading to the ranch, but his eyes watched her in the rearview mirror until she was gone from his sight.

13

What a difference a week makes.

Bianca was feeling good about her progress with the ranch and when she filled her father in during their brief conversation last night, even he had shown surprise. Kahron had suggested that the equipment was covered by the insurance on the barn and he was right, so Bianca put in a claim to the insurance company.

Although Bianca had a bone to pick with either Trishon or Papa Doc about discussing her father's rehab stint, the word was out that Hank King was trying to get his act together and that led to several of his clients actually calling *them* about doing business again.

Bianca signed the lease on the townhouse with her return to Holtsville and discovered she could move in whenever she chose. She would spend her first night in her sparsely furnished apartment tonight. She was more than happy not to listen to Trishon's backhanded comments on Kahron anymore. She would have her own space and escape that purple hell, just coming to work here at the ranch like a nine to fiver.

Harry was showing interest in buying her veterinary

practice. Susan and her husband were interested in the house. So, Bianca was in the process of getting both appraised for possible sales.

Bianca was even considering opening her clinic right here at the ranch. That was something she had to talk over with her father, so she put that idea on the back burner . . . for now.

Everything seemed to be flowing so well, falling right into place like puzzle pieces. Ever the pessimist, Bianca was waiting for the other shoe to drop.

"Busy as a bee."

Bianca looked up from the ad she was composing to go in the local paper to find Trishon strolling into the office. "I could use some help if you're offering," Bianca said, leaning back in her chair to watch her step-mother.

"The help I'm offering, you ain't takin'" she offered, moving to walk around the office.

"If you mean advice, your damn straight I'm not."

Trishon glanced at Bianca over her shoulder. "Your Daddy's not happy about you taking up with Kahron Strong."

Bianca released a heavy breath. "And that's something you felt the need to tell him while he's in rehab?" she asked, her voice tight.

"My husband and I have no secrets, Bianca."

Bianca returned her attention to the ad.

"It's a shame that something your supposed to be happy about, your hiding from your father."

Bianca eyes shifted to glare at the woman. "No, it's a shame that his wife would purposefully call him with an issue that can hinder his recovery."

"I have Hank's best interest in mind."

"And that's why you spent money like it was water

although you knew the business was struggling. That's why you set back and let him drink like a fish?"

Their eyes locked.

"Are you saying I married Hank for his money?" Trishon asked coldly.

"Damn straight I am," Bianca countered. "This is a whole different lifestyle from where you came from."

"You're a bitch, Bianca King."

"And you're a whore my father made into a housewife, and we all know how that goes."

Trishon stalked to the desk as if to strike Bianca.

Bianca rose from her chair to battle if necessary.

"At least I'm not a fool for Kahron Strong. Throwing yourself at him like you're begging to be screwed. The whole town's laughing at you trying to rebuild this ranch while your boyfriend sluts all over town and is trying to ruin the very thing your trying to build."

"I am so glad I have my own place because I am tired of looking at you and listening to the garbage you're always talking," Bianca spat.

"Hank and I need *our* home to *ourselves* anyway, so I'm just as happy as you are."

"Alcohol has been clouding my father's view of you for the last fifteen years." Bianca leaned forward to stick her face in Trishon's. "Without those liquor goggles I wonder what he'll think of you."

Bianca hit a sore spot. She saw the flash of fear and uncertainty in Trishon's eyes.

Kahron strolled into the office. "B, I got a surprise for you outside."

Trishon whirled on him, her face filled with rage. "I can't believe you keep showing your face around here while you're trying to ruin my husband," she yelled.

Bianca came around the desk to stand in front of Trishon

as the woman advanced on Kahron. "Slow your roll, Trishon," Bianca told her in hard, uncompromising tones.

Trishon's angry eyes shifted to Bianca in disbelief. "I can't believe you're choosing him over your father, because that is *exactly* what you're doing?" she said in a harsh and low whisper.

"Trishon, my father is wrong about Kahron, and so are you," Bianca insisted.

"When it all comes out how he's making a fool out your ass I will be the first one to laugh in your face." Trishon brushed past Bianca and nearly spent Kahron as she knocked her elbow into his arm.

"She still spouting that b–s about me, huh?"

Bianca nodded, fearing that her father was as vehement about Kahron as Trishon. She rubbed her brows with her fingers, hoping to hold off the tension she felt creeping up.

"I don't care what Trishon thinks," Bianca said, letting Kahron pull her into his arms.

"But what about your father?"

Bianca shrugged, wrapping her arms around Kahron's waist to hold him tighter. "He'll come around."

"And if he doesn't?"

Bianca tilted her head back to look up at Kahron because of his serious tone.

"It's important to me that you do believe me and trust me, B."

"Well I do."

Kahron shifted his hand up to lightly grasp Bianca's head, pulling it closer to him so that his tongue could plunge into her mouth with heat and circle her tongue the way he knew she loved.

Bianca grunted softly in pleasure, her hand dropping

to sit comfortably in his back pockets as she massaged his buttocks.

He ended the kiss with one last press of his lips to hers, playfully swatting her bottom. "I have to ride to Walterboro. Wanna go?" he asked.

"Let's ride. I can drop this ad to the paper while we're there."

Bianca followed Kahron out the house, climbing up into his truck.

"Let's have lunch first," he said, glancing at her before he accelerated the truck forward.

"Fine with me."

Bianca took calls on her cell from the appraisers she hired back in Atlanta, jotting down information in her address book. She was so busy asking questions that she didn't notice where Kahron had driven her until the truck came to a stop before one of the largest and most beautiful homes Bianca had ever laid eyes on.

"Can I get back to you? Thanks." Bianca closed the phone. "Where are we?"

"Strong Ranch," Kahron told her with pride as he climbed out of the truck.

Bianca loved the way nearly every space of the spacious brick home was glass. The lawn was well manicured with topiaries, well-trimmed bushes, and beautiful floral arrangements. The entire front yard was asphalt and the perimeter of the property was surrounded by a black wrought-iron fence.

She turned to look at Kahron in disbelief as he opened the passenger door. "Kahron, my hair's in a ponytail and I have on sweats. I didn't put on any make-up," she protested, even as she climbed out of the truck.

"You look beautiful, B." He smiled down at her.

"Yeah, whatever," she told him, pulling a compact out

of her purse to check that she was at least presentable. "You dead wrong for this."

A tall, slender woman of middle age stepped out onto the porch. "Kahron?" she called out.

He grabbed Bianca's hand as they made their way up the walkway to the porch.

"You must be, Dr. King," Mrs. Strong said, pulling her into a warm hug as soon as Bianca reached the top step.

Mrs. Strong smelled of vanilla, wise advice, home cooked meals, and that unconditional love only a mother could give. Bianca hugged her back, rapidly blinking away the tears she felt for the loss of her own mother before they could fall.

"Call me Bianca," she offered.

"What a pretty name," Mrs. Strong said, as they all entered the house. "Way too pretty for Kahron to call you by a letter."

They entered the dining room and any words Bianca thought of saying evaporated as four silver haired men immediately stood. They all looked like Kahron in some fashion—all tall and strong and handsome.

It was a little overwhelming.

Kahron must have saw it in her eyes because he took her hand in his and squeezed it reassuringly as he made the introductions. "This is my father, Kael."

"Nice to meet you, Dr. King."

"Biana," she softly corrected.

"And my oldest brother, Kade."

"So you're the one who has my brother's nose wide opened, huh?"

"I wouldn't say that." She smiled.

"And this is Kaleb."

Kaleb winked at her and smiled, showing a twin set

of dimples deep enough to drink out of. "Prettiest damn vet I ever seen, that's for sure."

"Slow your roll, little brother."

Everyone laughed.

"Well thank you, Kaleb," she responded, trying to memorize the name with each handsome face.

"And I'm Kaeden."

"You're the money man, right?" she asked with a smile as he shook her hand.

"That's me," he said, looking almost identical to Kahron, save for the spectacles he wore. "Kahron told us what you're doing at your father's ranch, just let me know if I can help at all."

"Thank you," she said in genuine surprise and pleasure. "I will do just that."

"Enough of the introductions, fellas, let's eat," Mrs. Strong said, setting a platter of homemade roast beef sandwiches and a tureen of vegetable soup on the table.

"Where's your sister?" Bianca asked as she and Kahron set to the table.

"Cancun with her girlfriends."

Bianca watched as the men dug into the food with gusto. She took a bite of the sandwich Kahron set on her plate and nearly stomped her foot at how good it was. "Mrs. Strong, this is sooooooo good," she sighed, wiping a bit of gravy from the corner of her mouth with her finger.

"Thank you." Mrs. Strong took a seat to the left of her husband. "Before I was married I used to run my own catering business in Savannah. Now I just cook for my boys."

"Well I can see why none of them married with you . . ."

Bianca's words trailed off at the expressions on everyone's faces. She didn't know what she said, but the taste of her foot was strong as everyone looked uncomfortable.

"Don't make her feel bad," Kade offered. "She had no way of knowing."

Bianca's eyes shifted to him.

"I was married once, but she . . . she—" he cleared his throat briefly—"she died last year."

Bianca reached out and squeezed Kade's hand. "I'm sorry, Kade."

He smiled at her but it didn't reach his eyes—sadness filled them instead. "It's okay," he reassured her.

Kahron squeezed her thigh and patted it warmly.

"Kade's daughter Kadina has the whole family in the palm of her hand," Kahron added, changing the subject.

Bianca smiled warmly. "I wish I could've met her."

"She's at school or trust me she would've made herself known," Kade mused.

"Bianca, Kahron says you're planning to move your practice to Holtsville?" Kael asked.

"Yes, I really would love to incorporate it right into the horse ranch, but I'll have to talk it over with my father and see what he says about it. That way I can serve as the vet on staff for the horse ranch for our boarders and still service others in the area."

"I think that's a good idea," Kaeden offered.

"My girl has a good head on her shoulders," Kahron bragged, winking at her. "She's really turning things around at her father's ranch."

"So are you scouting for land elsewhere to expand your business?" his father asked him.

"No, not yet."

Bianca stiffened. Somehow she always felt as if her success at revitalizing her father's ranch was in direct competition with Kahron furthering his dreams of expansion. Every time she was reminded of that her father's words came to her in a rush like a dry whisper—no matter how much she tried to forget them.

He wants my land.

Late that night, after finishing up all the work she was going to for the day, Bianca climbed the stairs to retrieve the last of her clothing from the room she now called "Prince's Purple Passion Pit" in lieu of the entertainer's well-known fondness for the color.

Trishon—who was now officially no longer speaking to Bianca—had retired to bed and the house was quiet and still.

Bianca was anxious to get her things and hightail it to scoop up Kahron, who was spending the first night in her new apartment with her—of course. She closed the dresser with her hip as she carried her handful of her undergarments to the open duffel on the bed.

She froze, her head cocking a little toward the window at a sudden noise that was different from the cry of night creatures. Dropping the garments on her bed she made her way to the window. Bianca used the purple polyester curtains to shield her as she peeked down to the yard below.

She gasped and her heart raced as a dark shadowy figure passed by the bushes.

Reacting on a impulse she dashed from the room and made her way down the stairs and out the door in record time. The figure shot into the trees lining the road and Bianca took off behind him.

"Enough is enough," she said, like a actress in a Lifetime movie.

She lurched forward at his back in the darkness, the

thick grove of trees even blocking any illumination from the moonlight. Bianca landed on her stomach hard enough to knock the air out of her with an "umf." She reached out just enough to catch one sneakered foot and the figure tripped, cursing as he landed hard.

She dragged herself up the length of his slender body by his clothes. "I got your ass," she said with effort as she also struggled to regain her breath.

The figure tried to roll over to get her off his back, but Bianca pressed all her weight upon him as she snaked her arm around his neck tightly.

The sound of feet pressed to grass echoed behind her and Bianca felt her first rush of fear. *Oh God, no. There's two of them.* Before she could turn her head to look over her shoulder she felt a sharp object brought roughly down upon the back of her head.

Her grasp around his neck slackened and she felt her limp body roughly rolled over into the grass as he rose. Her eyes felt heavy—too heavy to open—and she couldn't muster the will to cry as she felt herself spiraling into a dark abyss where even her pain and gripping fear didn't register.

Kahron finished throwing a change of clothes in a duffel bag, walking into his bathroom to grab his grooming products. Once that was done, he walked out of his bedroom with the bag and dropped it by the door. He was ready for Bianca to pick him up.

He smiled as he thought of her excitement over her first night in a townhouse—although beautiful and stylish— that was less than a third the size of her home in Atlanta.

That was Bianca. There was nothing pretentious

about her, and that was one of the many facets of her characters that he loved—liked . . . liked a lot.

Okay, loved. Yes, he loved Bianca.

Kahron's smile broadened at that thought. He welcomed it. Cherished it. Of course, with time the love would deepen and ripen, but yes, the seed had been planted in his heart.

He went into the kitchen to check on the chili Garcelle left for dinner. He and Bianca would eat here and then head to Walterboro. He turned the pot off as the food steamed when he lifted the top.

Kahron glanced down at his watch, moving to his living room to flip absentmindedly through the channels. Hershey's head lifted at the sight of him and she moved to stand beside him. "Hey girl," he said, scratching her shiny coat as he settled on the large comfortable sofa with a yawn.

Three hours later he awoke with a start. Even Hershey slept on the floor beside him. Kahron wiped his mouth with his hands as he moved to sit up. He frowned at the time. *Where is she?*

He reached for his phone and tried her cell number twice before hanging up. Then he tried the house number.

"Hello."

"Trishon, is Bianca there?" he asked, pressing the mute button on the remote to silence the television.

"Fuck you." She hung up.

Kahron grabbed his keys and left the house.

Bianca had no clue to time nor place as she slowly stirred to consciousness. She opened her eyes but closed them as the dark shadow of trees swirled around her like she was on a merry-go-round. Slowly, it all came back to her. The noise. The shadow. The trees. The chase.

She just thanked God they left her to live.

Bianca grunted and winced at the sharp dart of pain that assailed her when she tried to lift her head from where it pressed into the soft earth. *Get up, Bianca. Get up.*

She pressed her palms into the ground and lifted up her upper body, only for her arms to tremble and then give out beneath her. "Aah," she cried out as the action caused her head to rage.

With effort she raised her hand and gingerly touched the back of her head. The warm, stickiness of blood coated her fingers. She had to swallow back down the contents of her stomach.

Her determination rose.

There was no way she was going to lay here and die.

He longed to rest his leg. He couldn't go home. Not now. People would see his injuries and wonder where they come from. When Bianca tripped him, he fell down hard on his knees and already he felt them swelling and throbbing with pain. His forehead had scraped a tree limb and there was an ugly gash remaining.

His cell phone continued its incessant ringing as he tried his best to stretch out across the cab of the truck. He ignored it. Their plans and their schemes would have to wait.

Kahron banged on the front door and rang the doorbell all at once. What had started as a polite knock from a neighbor increased in weight and occurrence as his

knocks went ignored. It took another round of knocks
and ringing before he heard the door unlock.

"Have you lost your mind, Kahron Strong?" Trishon
snapped, standing there in a nightie that was far too
revealing to open a door in.

He breezed past her and walked into the house.
"Where's Bianca?" he asked, walking to the office only
to find it empty.

"Get the hell out of here, Kahron, or I'll call the
police."

He headed up the stairs and opened each of the doors,
pausing in a purple room where Bianca's opened duffel
bag sat in the middle of the bed.

Kahron left the room and jogged back down the
stairs. "Where is Bianca?" he roared into Trishon's face.

"I don't know," Trishon answered. "What part of that
don't you understand?"

Kahron was worried, and the last thing he needed was
Trishon's attitude. He grabbed her shoulders and peered
down at her with hard and angry eyes. "Trishon, now's
not the time nor place for your bullshit. When did you
last see Bianca?"

She stared at him long and hard before she answered.
"When I went to bed she was in her room packing. I've
been sleep ever since so I don't have a clue what all this
is about."

He released her and strode out the door. He stood
there, hands on his narrow hips, as he prayed he was just
overreacting.

Bianca crawled like a dog on its belly across the dirt,
grass, rough tree limbs, trying desperately to reach the
edge of the trees. Every time she tried to muster the

will to rise, she would fall. Every time she felt defeated and wanted to give up, she became twice as determined than before.

Her tears flowed with the dirt on her face, and she could taste it in her mouth. Pain made her body shake and tremble as she sweated with each torturous movement.

She didn't care. The tears, the pain, and the sweat meant she was still alive.

His cell phone rang and it jarred him from his sleep. He winced as he shifted to comfort. It felt like someone was digging a large and sharp knife into his knee.

Knowing the ringing wouldn't stop, he snatched up the cell phone. "What?" he snapped.

"Make the call."

His breathing was jagged and the smell of his own sweat and grime filled the interior of the truck. "Huh?"

"Make the damn call!"

The line went dead.

He was sick of them and their demands. Their orders. Like he was a flunkey in their game. Do this. Do that. Go here. Go there.

But, he was in too deep now to stop. He thought of Bianca's lifeless body and wondered if she was dead or alive.

Pushing away his guilt, he dialed the number, squinting in the darkness to see the numbers.

Kahron checked every bit of the ranch he could think of, but he still couldn't find her. Even Trishon had set aside her anger and helped him search—now that she saw his concern for Bianca's welfare may be valid.

He walked up from the barn, having checked that twice as if his eyes deceived him the first time. No sign of her.

Something was wrong. He knew that as good as he knew his own name.

He reached for his cell phone, but remembered it was on the passenger seat of his pick-up truck. He had reached his truck and was dialing the number for the police when he heard a noise behind him.

He whirled around, his eyes darting to every inch of the property. He stopped, his body froze in its stance as he listened for the sound again.

"Kahron."

His breath caught as he heard it again. His head swung to the trees.

"Kahron . . . please . . . help me."

He ran to the trees, his heart pounding, fear nearly chocking him. As he neared the edge of the trees that had once served as their playground, he saw Bianca's prone figure crawling forward.

"Bianca," he cried out hoarsely, sliding to the ground beside her to gather her into his arms.

Kahron ached as she cried out in pain. "I got you baby. I got you," he told her as he rose to his feet with her securely in his arms. He walked as quickly as he could to his truck, trying not to jar her.

Trishon stepped out onto the porch and her eyes took in Bianca's limp and dirty body. Her screams pierced the night.

Bianca eyes opened slowly and became focused. She looked around, wincing a bit with the movement. She was in a hospital room. Her clothes hung in the mini-closet by the sink. The sun beamed through the window, telling of morning. Kahron slept by her head, his head nearly falling off of the fist on which it sat.

She shivered at the idea that she lay unconscious in the woods for hours before she had to claw her way to the edge to beg pitifully for help. She blinked away the tears.

Someone left her to die last night and that was a lot to swallow.

As she lay in the darkness she thought of her father, Kahron, Mimi, even Armand, her accomplishments, her goals . . . her life. She wept for them all. She begged to have them all back.

It was foolish of her to take on the roll of vigilante.

"Hey you."

Gingerly, she turned her head on the pillow, smiling as Kahron sat forward to lean in close to her. "Hey," she said, her voice sounding hoarse and odd to her own ears.

He gathered her hands into his and pressed his lips to her fingers. His eyes searched hers, filled with emotion that made Bianca completely breathless.

"I thought I lost you," he told her huskily, reaching forward to brush her hair from her face.

Bianca smiled, her own eyes glistening a bit. "I'm okay, Kahron. Feeling stupid, but okay."

The hospital room door opened and Trishon walked in, followed by two police officers.

"Do I need to be alone to give my statement?" Bianca asked, her thumb massaging Kahron's hand. "I really want him to stay."

Trishon stepped aside as the taller of the officers stepped forward. "Actually were not here for your statement, ma'am."

Bianca looked to Kahron—who frowned, and then to Trishon—who looked pleased.

"Well why *are* you here?" Kahron asked, his face pensive as he looked up at them.

"We have some new developments in the theft of the equipment from the ranch—"

"This couldn't wait?" Kahron asked.

"Obviously not."

Bianca held up her hands. "Listen, Kahron, baby, it's okay," she told him. "I want to hear this."

"Actually, ma'am, we wanted to talk to Mr. Strong."

Both Bianca and Kahron looked confused and asked, "Why?"

"Based on a tip we received last night, we acquired a search warrant and discovered the stolen property on your premises, Mr. Strong." The shorter officer stepped forward.

Bianca released Kahron's hand.

Kahron jumped to his feet. "You got to be kidding me."

"I told you, it was him, but you wouldn't listen," Trishon screeched from behind the police officer.

"Mr. Strong, if you'll come with us, we have some questions for you."

"This is some real bullshit." Kahron stiffened his shoulders as one of the police officers stepped closer to him.

Snippets and tidbits of words, comments, and conversations came flooding back to Bianca. Was Kahron, *her* Kahron, behind all of this all the while?

Around the same time he started making offers to buy me out somebody's been pulling shenanigans around my damn ranch.

"Lock his ass up," she heard Trishon say.

"Bianca, I know you don't believe this," she heard Kahron say.

He had the audacity to tell me I could either sell it to him outright or he'd get it one way or another eventually.

"Come with us, Mr. Strong."

"Bianca . . . B . . . say something, B."

She looked up, the confusion she felt written all over his face.

I promise you I haven't done anything to sabotage your father's business.

She wiped her face with her hands as one officer placed a hand on Kahron's elbow and steered him out the room. Kharon's eyes were locked on her even as he walked away.

It's not you that I don't have the faith in, Bianca.

"Told you he wasn't no good. I told you. I told you," Trishon said, with way too much glee.

Was all of it a ploy to get some damn land? All of Bianca's doubts plagued her. What if Kahron was making a fool out of her? She really didn't know him. It had been less than a month since he first caught her eye on the highway.

It felt like much longer.

You can trust me, Bianca.

"See ya. Wouldn't wanna be ya." Trishon waved Kahron away.

Bianca met his eyes again just before the door closed behind him.

Trust is very important to me, B.

14

Bianca picked up the phone but dropped it back like it was on fire. She had this inner struggle every day, nearly a hundred times a day. Call Kahron or not? Which to her was the same as trust Kahron or not.

Lord she missed him.

This last week seemed like an eternity without him.

But she was conflicted.

The police had actually arrested Kahron for possession of stolen property. She already knew his family posted bail the very next day, but she didn't call him and he didn't bother to call her.

It was over.

With Kahron's arrest came other issues. Was he behind the vandalism on her car as well? The attack she suffered last week? Maybe her father hadn't been wrong and the barn *was* burned down.

She trusted Kahron in her home, her bed . . . her heart. All the while he was plotting to destroy the work she put into the ranch for some land?

Her fingers sought and found the jagged stitches at the back of her head.

In truth she found it hard to believe Kahron would be behind physically hurting her. Was she stupid or what?

So, her feelings of doubt wavered with her feelings of anger at him. The anger usually won out. He said he wasn't involved, but why was the stolen equipment found in the shed where he kept his muscle car? Had the same hounds who stole the equipment for him attacked her to keep her from finding out their identity?

Why hadn't he contacted her to defend his innocence?

Bianca released a heavy breath, and pulled out the accordion folder of her father's files. She'd been meaning to go through them since she first arrived. She wanted to get his office organized before his arrival home next week. Besides, keeping busy kept her mind off Kahron.

So, even though she felt like dropping her head to the desk and bawling like a baby she blinked away the tears, swallowed back the pain, and focused on the hundred of papers and forms in front of her on the desk.

She separated them into piles: TRASH, IMPORTANT, ASK DADDY. She dropped most of the tattered and worn papers into the trash pile, shaking her head at the stack of warranty papers for appliances she knew they no longer owned. She placed quite a few small insurance policies that she needed to check the status of in the ASK DADDY pile.

"Deed and title. Ranch contracts. Old flyers. Prenuptial papers. Old light bills . . ."

Prenup? Bianca paused, her eyebrow arching as her fingers sought and found the legal document. She read it quickly, ending with her father and Trishon's signatures. "Well at least Daddy had sense to do that," she muttered, putting it in the IMPORTANT pile.

Bianca continued through each paper until it was all sorted. She took the stack of important papers and put them back in the accordion file. The other stacks she left to take care of later.

Today she was going to help the ranch hands with the daily turnout of the three horses she purchased from North Carolina. Her father was excited at the prospect of getting home to start training them. Bianca rose, grabbing the sexy pink Stetson she brought, before walking to the door.

The phone rang once. She turned to pick it up but the ringing ended abruptly. Shrugging, she left the office.

Kahron dropped the phone after just one ring. As badly as he wanted to hear Bianca's voice, feel her body in his arms, and have her back in his life, Kahron was determined not to call her. He would not make the first move to beg her forgiveness for something he didn't do. Something she should *know* he didn't do.

Sure, he looked guilty . . . but he wasn't. It hurt him that she automatically believed the worst in him. She had no faith in him. No trust.

He had more to deal with than Bianca, though. Someone set him up and Kahron was on a mission to find the culprit. He checked in with the unofficial "street committee," but so far no gossip concerning the matter had surfaced.

There was one thing he knew for sure. Someone working here at the ranch—*his* ranch—had to be in on it. How else could someone sneak all that equipment on his property without being caught. Possible? Yes. Improbable? Definitely.

Kahron looked up as his brothers Kade and Kaeden walked into his office. "Whassup, ya'll."

Kaeden removed his spectacles to clean with his

handkerchief. "We're on our way to Charleston and stopped by to check up on you," he said.

Kade frowned as he looked at Kaeden in disbelief. "Real subtle."

"What?" Kaeden asked.

Kade just shook his head.

"I don't need to be checked up on," Kahron insisted. "I been arrested, my girlfriend—uh, ex-girlfriend—has given me her ass to kiss, and someone's setting me up . . . *but* I don't need to be checked on."

Kade and Kaeden shared a long look.

"Any ideas?" Kade asked.

Kahron leaned back in his chair, his hand stroking his silver shadow as he gazed out the open window with pensive eyes. "The only thing I keep coming back to is the King land, but nothing makes sense."

"I agree somebody wants it to look like you want the land no matter what. Question is why? Hell, King already said he wasn't selling it to you, and finding out you stole from him isn't going to help that," Kaeden offered, folding his tall frame into one of the club chairs before Kahron's desk.

"That's the same part my brain gets stuck on," Kahron said.

"So you haven't talked to Bianca yet?" Kade asked, running his fingers through his thick curls as he sat on the edge of his brother's desk.

"No."

Kade and Kaeden exchanged another look.

"Must be really hard for Bianca—"

"What!" Kahron exclaimed, cutting off Kaeden's words.

"Call her. Talk to her," Kade encouraged.

"She didn't call me and I damn sure ain't calling her,"

Kahron insisted, picking up a pen only to throw it down in disgust.

"You always are stubborn like Pops," Kaeden added.

Kade nodded in agreement.

Kahron looked at them both like they were crazy.

"Just put yourself in Bianca's shoes. I wouldn't know what to think either, man," Kade told him.

"Do you think I stole the equipment?" Kahron asked, looking first to Kade and then Kaeden. "Do you?"

"Hell naw," they both answered without hesitation.

"But all the evidence points to me, so . . . why don't ya'll believe it?"

Kade and Kaeden exchanged a long look.

"Come on, Kahron. I see the point your getting it at but—"

"But hell," Kahron stressed. "I opened myself up to this woman. I told her secrets. I shared my dreams, my hopes, my everything with her. And after all that she can just turn her back on me like I was crap on her shoe? To hell with Bianca King."

"Just seems to me you were happier with her than without her, and that means something in my book," Kade said in a low voice.

"And trust is something in mine," Kahron countered, in a voice that was nearly identical to his brother.

Kahron and Kade locked eyes but there was nothing but brotherly concern and love in the depths.

"Just promise me I'll be best man at the wedding," Kade said with the hint of a smile at his lips.

"Did I not just say to hell with Bianca King?" Kahron asked in exasperation.

Kade reached into his back pocket of his Dickies pants for his wallet and pulled out a crisp one hundred dollar bill to toss on Kahron's desk. "That says you and

Bianca will be sniffing back around each other by next week," he said with confidence.

"I want a piece of that," Kaeden added, tossing two fifties onto the desk as well.

"Oh, so that's how ya'll gone play me?"

Kade and Kaeden looked at each other and then looked at Kahron. "Yup."

Trishon was taking a hot bubble bath scented with apples when Hank made his ritual nightly call. Like clockwork the phone rang at 8 P.M.

"Hey baby," she purred, playing in the bubbles.

"Hi Trishon."

"I miss you so much, Hank."

"Yeah, me too."

"I'm going to throw you a big welcome home party next week."

"Uhm, well, maybe you should hold off from that. I don't want to be around people drinking right now."

"Don't be silly, Hank."

He remained quiet.

"This is the longest we've ever been apart."

"Yeah, I know. Bianca there?"

Trishon frowned at the change of conversation. "She went home."

"I have to talk to her so I better call her."

She felt his distance and her brow wrinkled with worry.

"Hank," she called out suddenly, biting her thumb nail as she sat up in the water.

"Yes, Trishon?"

"I love you, Hank," she said, needing to feel her power. Silence.

"Hank?"

"Yeah, me too, Trish. Me too. Okay."

Her eyes glittered like cold diamonds. "Pap Doc said to call him ASAP. Something 'bout it being important."

"I'll call right after I talk to Bianca."

"Hank?"

"What, Trishon? What?"

"Nothing. Not a damn thing."

They hung up at the same time.

Bianca eyed her slightly ajar front door of her townhouse. She used her foot to swing the door open, but she didn't step over the threshold. The light from the porch framed her in the doorway as she reached inside to flip the light switch and illuminate the room.

Her knees weakened and fear clutched at her heart like a vice. Bianca took an involuntary step back as her wide eyes took in the scene before her.

Her home was a shambles. A mess. A deliberate and diabolical mess.

Furniture was turned upside down. The glass of her tables was shattered. Potted plants torn to shreds. Pictures destroyed and broken in half.

"What the hell?" she shrieked, reaching in her purse for her cell phone.

She quickly moved back to the parking lot, hating that her first instinct was to run and hide. Fear never set well with her, but after her attack last week—among the trees she once thought of as a haven—she was no longer falling for the okey-doke and putting herself in danger.

She made the call to the police, staying planted by her car even as her eyes took in the destruction inside her living room.

What the hell had she gotten herself into?

This was about more than the damn land. Someone wanted her gone and that was completely clear. All of it was muddling her brains. The shenanigans at the farm. The stolen equipment. The vandalism on her car. Her attack last week. Now this. All of it lay in jagged pieces that would eventually fit like pieces of a puzzle so that the picture of someone's intent would be clear.

Even the attempt to make Kahron look guilty.

Yes, whoever the culprit was had pushed their hand too far. This last attempt did not reinforce her belief in Kahron's guilt. It made her even more clear that someone was setting him up.

What would Kahron gain by scaring her back to Atlanta when he was one of the reasons she moved back to Holtsville? *Maybe he just wants me to think he wanted you here?*

No, Bianca, she argued with herself as she paced before her car. *Stop second guessing him. Stop doubting him. Stop it.*

If Kahron wanted the land, stealing the equipment and then leaving it on his ranch was not the smartest move at all. The theft made him less likely to get the land, and that was ultimately Kahron's well-admitted goal. The land.

Bianca was still pacing and thinking, trying to be clear. Trying to think clear. Use rationale. Discard foolishness. Embrace reason.

"Think. Make sense, B." She paused at her own use of Kahron's nickname for her. An endearment. Something brought forth from caring.

Trust is very important to me, B.

"Dr. King?"

Bianca whirled to find two police officers walking up to her. She shook each of their warm hands. "Yes."

"You got one helluva enemy, ma'am? This is your fourth incident in a month."

She locked eyes with the officer. "Yes, I do, and I'm gonna find out just who the hell it is."

"Brrrnnnggg."

Kahron was jolted from sleep where he lounged on the sofa with the television watching him more than he was watching it. He reached on the floor for his cordless. "Yo."

"I need your help."

Kahron's heart hammered in his chest at the sound of Bianca's voice. He felt like the very breath was knocked from him. After nearly seven days without her voice, it was rain during a drought. Needed. Wanted. Prayed for.

He hated to admit that.

"Why are you calling me, Bianca?" he asked forcing hardness to his voice.

"I told you. I need your help."

He frowned as he wiped his mouth, his fingers smoothing the fine hairs of his slight beard. "Is that all you have to say to me?"

"No . . . no, not at all." She released a breath. "But what I have to say to you has to be said in person."

"Where are you, B? I mean Bianca?"

"So I'm not B anymore?"

"B would have trusted me. There is no B, you're just Bianca. Now where are you?"

"Open the door."

His head turned to the closed door. He kept the phone pressed to his face even as he rose from the couch and walked bare-chested to the door. He inhaled and then exhaled as he opened it and found Bianca standing before him, her cell phone pressed to her face as well.

Urges, needs, and wants filled him with intensity. He fought them. No hugs, no kisses, no words whispered of how much he missed her . . . and loved her. He felt betrayed. He wanted his heart to stay cold.

"Well, what you got to say, Bianca?" he asked, cutting off the phone as he heard Hershey walk up to them.

"Someone broke into my townhouse today—"

Kahron laughed in derision and flung his hands up into the air as he stepped onto the porch. "Yeah, I guess I was at your door like a crackhead with a butter knife jimmying your door right? Why would I think you were here being woman enough to admit that you were wrong to believe I would ever hurt you, B. Why? This isn't about some damn land. This is about you and me. And you should know damn well I wouldn't hurt you in any way. I was wrong about you before and you know what—tonight is no exception."

Bianca bit her lip as she looked to the moon as if she was counting to ten. "Are you done?" she asked, sounding a little irritable.

"Hell no," he said with emphasis, starting to pace in his bare feet. "I've been waiting a week to get this off my chest."

Bianca released a heavy breath and moved to sit down on the top step of his stairs. "I know damn well you didn't break into my apartment today. Just like I know you didn't have anything to do with the equipment that was stolen. But I'm gone cop a squat. Looks like you got a lot to say."

And just like that he felt foolish, which made him

angry. "Bianca, what . . . what the hell you want, huh? Wh–wh–what–what?"

Bianca leaned back against the porch rail and looked up at him. "I'm sorry. I was wrong. I made a mistake. I picked the wrong box. I took the wrong road at the fork. I chose the wrong hand. *Damn,* Kahron. I f'ed up, okay. I get it. If you can't forgive me for looking out for me, first and foremost, and taking a pause to make sure I wasn't getting played, then that's fine, but right now I need your help."

Kahron braced his hands on the rail, leaning forward. "You weren't there when they broke in, we're you?" he asked, unable to fight the concern he felt for her.

Bianca rose, moving to stand beside him. "No, I wasn't, but they tore it up pretty good."

Kahron looked down at her. "I'm glad you weren't hurt, B," he said in a low voice.

"Me too, which is why I want to get on the offense and not the defense. Maybe if we sort this mess out together we can both benefit."

Kahron nodded. "I was thinking along the same lines. The sooner we find just who the hell is behind all this the sooner I know you'll be safe and I can prove to the police that I'm innocent."

They fell silent, but Kahron's eyes saw the defeat in Bianca's shoulders and just a touch of that old sadness about her eyes. She turned as if she felt his eyes on her, and he couldn't look away from those amazing hazel eyes to save his life.

He saw the same hunger he felt for her and he knew that all he had to do was to pull Bianca into his arms and she would be back in his life. Just like that.

But he didn't reach for her.

Bianca blinked rapidly.

"You're not going back to Walterboro tonight are you?" he asked.

"Oh no. I'm not sleeping in that place until I get some sturdier locks that more than a hard shoulder can outdo."

Kahron smiled at her ability to find any humor in the situation. "You're welcome to stay here," he offered.

"That wasn't my intention in coming here tonight."

He nodded. "I know."

Bianca stepped closer to him. "But I'll be honest."

Kahron's heart raced as Bianca raised her hand to lovingly stroke his chin. One simple touch and his body betrayed him as he inhaled deeply of her scent—one he knew so well.

"I want my man back. My friend back. My lover back. My heart and soul back," Bianca whispered. "Now *that* is my intention."

Kahron resolve was undone. He raised his own hands to lightly grasp Bianca's smooth cinnamon face. "Can I be honest?"

"Please."

"I'm glad you're not as stubborn as me."

Their bodies melted against one another with ease. Arms encased bodies. Pelvis pressed together. Moans mingled. Tongues dances as they kissed first passionately and then feverishly. Their hearts beat with a unified rhythm.

Hershey circled them where they stood, the sound of her breathing mingling with their moans of pleasure.

"I think your bitch is jealous," Bianca teased softly against his softly bearded cheek.

Kahron laughed, his body shaking as he held her closer.

* * *

Sometimes in life the mind locks away a minute detail. Something so seemingly insignificant that it's almost forgotten. Just when its least expected a light bulb brightens, the key to that locked door of the brain clicks open. As that door opens other snippets of seemingly innocent comments or events are recalled with a domino effect. One leads to the other and other and the other. Sometimes the "click" happens for no reason at all, and other times there's an event or a person that nudges the door open.

It happened for Bianca somewhere around 2 A.M. that morning. Naked and sated by the physical and emotional reunion with Kahron, Bianca was sitting in the window pane of his bedroom when she saw a lone figure limp across the front yard and enter the bunkhouse.

A lone and familiar figure.

And just like that . . . *click*.

15

"I never thought I would be playing Mouse to your Easy Rawlins, B."

Bianca smile was cloaked by the darkness of the woods where she and Kahron sat on one of his four wheelers in the grove of trees. "We planted the trap yesterday now let's just see who falls into it."

"I understand that, but there's a thousand other things we could doing," he said throatily near her ear from behind her as his hands rose from her hips to deeply squeeze her breasts.

"Focus, Strong," she told him dryly.

Kahron rolled her nipples between his fingers. "Trust me, I'm focused."

Bianca laughed and tried half-heartedly to brush his tempting fingers away. "Don't start something we can't finish."

Kahron nuzzled her nape. "This four wheeler is sturdy. We can finish."

Twin lights suddenly beamed from the head of the long road.

Kahron's hand fell away and Bianca felt his heart thunder against her back, mirroring her own.

Bianca eyes locked on a small break in the trunk of the towering trees. "Here we go."

Trishon sprayed her favorite perfume, Pleasures by Estee Lauder, over every inch of her nude body before slipping on a sheer ivory robe that concealed nothing . . . just the way she wanted.

She was just heading down the stairs when the doorbell sounded. She smiled and it was like that of a kitten being stroked or of a kitten about to be stroked. She peeked out the window before opening the door wide.

"Hi lover," she purred, enjoying the way his eyes traveled up and down her nude frame.

Dante pulled her into arms, kissing her deeply as he kicked the door closed with his foot. "How's my Kitten?" he asked.

"Better now that you're here."

Dante was the man that gave Trishon the sexual satisfaction that she craved. Her appetite was strong, and Hank King had long since stopped sating her.

Trishon made him release her and dropped to unbutton his pants and release his tool, she licked her lips greedily before taking him deeply into her mouth and throat with skill and ease as she squatted before him.

"Damn," he swore, throwing his head back as his hand tightly held a fistful of her hair.

Trishon didn't stop until she felt his thighs quiver and his member stiffen. Soon his seed filled her mouth and she swallowed it greedily, loving the pleasure she gave him, but more importantly the control she had over him.

Sex conquered all.

She looked up at him and released him with one final lick. "That's for all your help these weeks. Without you none of this would've worked."

Dante fell back against the wall, nearly tripping from his pants being down around his ankles. He said nothing as his member hung limp and drained between his thighs.

Trishon eyes squinted as she rose. "You know this has to stay our secret, don't you, Dante?" she asked.

He jerked his pants up around his waist and looked at her. "You think I want to go to jail for the all this shit I did for you?" he asked roughly. "Burning that barn is arson. Bianca's car. The stolen equipment I planted. All of that shit adds up to a lot of jail time I ain't even feeling. For *all* of us."

"Yes, but it worked, and we couldn't have done it without you."

Bianca and Kahron had left the four wheeler behind and made their way to the front of the grove of trees. They were just moving across the front yard to near the house when a twin pool of light shown from the head of the road again. They dashed to the side of the house, letting the darkness cloak them as they bent down.

Bianca was in the front and she leaned to the side just enough to see who drove the second vehicle. They hadn't been expecting anyone else and everything could be ruined.

She frowned at the crimson red of the truck.

Trishon and Dante froze as the headlights flashed against the wall. Dante peeked out the front window.

"What the hell is he doing here?" he asked, anger lacing his voice.

Trishon moved beside him and peeked out the window as well. "Oh shit. He can't find you here."

"Are you fucking him?" he asked, grabbing her wrist.

Trishon rolled her eyes heavenward. "Don't be silly. What I want with his old ass? Putting up with Hank is more than enough."

Dante gripped her chin tightly. "You better not be lying to me Trishon," he warned, his eyes angry and dangerous. "I didn't risk my ass for you behind no bullshit."

"Trust me, baby."

The grip on her chin slackened.

"Where did you park?"

"Behind the house."

Trishon pushed him towards the kitchen. "Go out that way and be careful."

The doorbell rang just as Dante slid out the side entrance to the kitchen.

The kitchen door opened and Kahron dashed behind the back of the house, pulling Bianca with him. He swore when he saw the work truck parked there. He motioned for Bianca to be quiet and move further back. He rose and pressed his body to the house right at the corner

Seconds later Dante tipped around the corner.

Under the dim light from the moon, Bianca saw his eyes round at the sight of Kahron standing there.

Kahron didn't give him change to speak, knocking him first in the stomach so hard that his body curved upward and then with an upper cut to his chin that sent him flying backwards.

Dante rose unsteadily and came lumbering back at Kahron.

Hoping to get help to subdue Dante she dashed around the house.

Trishon opened the door wide and smiled up at Papa Doc. "Hi lover," she said huskily, still dressed in nothing but her sheer robe, the taste of Dante's semen still heavy on her breath.

He smiled broadly, his gold tooth flashing against his broad teeth as he used one arm to jerk her naked body against him.

She kissed him, perversely thrilled that he had no idea that he tasted of her other lover's seed as he suckled her tongue.

Her attraction to Papa Doc was his money, but it was not nearly enough to compete with Hank's wealth when they first wed. Wealth he no longer had. Wealth she had no right to if they divorced. Wealth he would regain if he sold the ranch for the millions of dollars it was worth. Money she couldn't wait to spend.

Of course, she would never leave Hank, not for Dante nor Papa Doc—her husband's so called best friend. She couldn't afford to. But Papa Doc didn't care. He needed some of that money just as badly as she did, and she didn't mind sharing as long as he did what she told him. He was another of her pawns controlled by her sex.

The whole scheme to hire Dante to help "convince" Hank to sell had been her idea, but Papa Doc was her willing accomplice.

The first time she stroked his thigh under the dining

room table and she felt his swift hardness against her hands, she knew he was hers.

Men were so stupid.

Bianca blinked away the tears at knowing her father had been betrayed by his wife and his best friend as she made her way back to Kahron.

"Where's Papa Doc?" Kahron asked as he wrestled a battered Dante to his feet and held him securely by his forearms behind his back.

"He's in on it. I saw them at the front door kissing."

"Who?" Kahron and Dante asked in unison.

"Papa Doc and Trishon," she told them.

"I'll kill that bitch," Dante swore, trying to break free of Kahron's strong grasp and failing.

"Mad your partner in this b-s getting some of her stankness, too?" Bianca bitterly, fighting the urge to slap him.

"Call the police, B," Kahron said, still holding Dante's arms as he pushed him forward.

"I got it," she said, her heart still racing with adrenaline as she dialed the number she now knew by heart.

Papa Doc had his pants down around his pale ankles as he stood behind Trishon, his member planted deeply within her walls as she clutched the stairs.

"Harder, Daddy. Harder," she screamed curving her back as she wiggled her buttocks against him.

A cold draft breezed against his buttocks and the back of his thighs.

He turned and his eyes widened to find Bianca,

Kahron, a bruised Dante, and two police officers standing in the doorway.

He jumped back, his member sliding out of Trishon as he jerked his pants up.

"What you doing, Daddy?" Trishon purred, wiggling her bottom as she looked back over her shoulder.

Bianca stepped forward and lifted her foot to press against Trishon's behind before anyone could stop her.

Twenty minutes later, the police had everyone in Hank King's office as they tried to make heads or tails of the whole situation Bianca and Kahron laid out for them.

"So let me get this straight," Officer Kandor asked, looking down at his notes. "Mrs. King and Louis Redding—also known as Papa Doc—convinced Dante to vandalize her husband's ranch—including burning of the barn—so that he would sell his land to Mr. Kahron Strong here because the King business was failing and if she left him she would get nothing because of the prenuptial she signed."

He stopped and looked up at Kahron and Bianca who both sat on opposite edges of the desk. Each nodded.

"We just discovered Mr. Redding's involvement with Trishon tonight. Honestly, I don't know how deeply he's into it all. He could be a criminal or just a low-life son-of-a-bitch who was willing to stab his best friend in the back for a tramp." Bianca's anger at Papa Doc was clear.

"Your Mama's a tramp, trick," Trishon spat at her, her revealing nightgown covered by one of the police officer's blankets.

"Refrain from the profanity ladies," the officer by the door added.

Bianca help up her hand. "Sorry."

"Whatever," Trishon said with attitude.

Officer Kandor shifted his eyes back to his notepad. "Now Mr. King—who is in a rehab facility for alcoholism—called his daughter from Atlanta for help, and this throws a wrench in the plans because you, Miss King, started to turn the business around and Mr. King had no desire to sell. So to get rid of you, Mrs. King and Papa Doc hired Dante Mitchell to vandalize your car, steal the equipment and plant it at Mr. Strong's ranch—whom he works for—and break into your apartment."

"Yes," Kahron said. "Bianca was at my house and saw Dante returning to the bunkhouse early in the morning. She recognized his figure from the night of her assault. Once she suspected him she put it together that Dante was involved with Trishon."

"I saw a figure in the yard late one night before. Trishon told me it was her brother but everyone knows she has nothing at all to do with her family—including her own mother. It was Dante that night as well, wasn't it Trishon?"

Bianca and Trishon shared hateful glares.

Office Kandor nodded. "So you both let Mr. Mitchell and Mrs. King think you had returned to Atlanta and had no intention of returning or helping with the ranch."

"Yes," Kahron and Bianca said in unison.

"Now where are the tapes you told the dispatcher about?" Officer Kandor asked, sliding his notebook into the front pocket of his uniform.

Until then Trishon, Dante, and Papa Doc had looked bored and insolent.

"What tapes?" Trishon asked, her eyes burning with hatred as she glared at Bianca.

Bianca rose and smiled with sweet satisfaction. "When I came to the house for the last time a couple of days ago I planted little voice-activated tape recorders. Five in all. I'll get them."

She reached under the ledge of the desk and handed the small device taped there to the police officer. "That's one."

Bianca left the office and retrieved the others from the kitchen, the master bedroom, the porch, and lastly the foyer. She walked into the office and handed them all to Officer Kandor. "There must be something on one of these implicating them, especially this one from the foyer."

Office Kandor rewound the recorder and then pushed play.

Dante dropped his head as his voice clearly played as he admitted to burning the barn and the other incidents.

The officer fast forwarded through the sounds of their sex play as Papa Doc looked at Trishon is disbelief. She just stared ahead stoically.

"Hank called me like you said he would, but that bastard still won't sell the ranch even after I lined up a helluva deal with that rancher from Greenville. But at least Dante ran Bianca's ass off, and trust me Hank will have everything so f'ed up again he'll be begging to sell. He'll be back drinking if I have to pour it down his throat."

Bianca's eyes shifted to Papa Doc as his own words of betrayal and culpability echoed in the room.

She didn't hear the rest of his words—she didn't have to.

"You three are the biggest idiots I have ever seen because this is the dumbest scheme I've heard cooked up," Bianca told them as the police jerked them all to their feet and began to handcuff them. "But believe me, no weapons formed against my father shall prosper because he has me watching his damn back and at least now he can brush the dirt he called his wife and his best friend off his shoulder. Ya'll are pathetic."

"What a day," Kahron said, yawning as he climbed into his bed beside Bianca.

"I still can't believe people can be so conniving and so treacherous," Bianca sighed, curling her body along the length of Kahron's.

"How did your Dad take it?"

Bianca licked her lips. "I talked to his counselor and he suggested that I be upfront with him and tell him in person, so I'm driving down tomorrow."

"Honesty is always the best policy," Kahron admitted as he played with her finger. "Can I be honest with you?"

Bianca smiled. "Always."

"I love you."

Bianca tilted her head up to look up at him and meet his eyes with her own. "Tell me something I don't know," she told him softly.

Kahron rolled her onto her back and lay atop her between her open thighs. "You don't have to say it, B. It's written all over your face."

"Oh, please, that's gas," she teased, even as she stroked his beard lovingly.

Kahron tickled her until tears filled Bianca's eyes and she let out her hog like snort. "Okay, okay . . . okay."

He paused.

"I Bianca King love you Kahron Strong with every little piece of my heart," she told him sweetly, kissing his lips.

"Tell me something I *don't* know," he teased, rolling out of the bed as Bianca reached for a pillow to swing at him.

Epilogue

One Year Later

Bianca smiled up at her father as she took her place by his side and offered her his arm in his handsome tuxedo. "Ready, Daddy?"

He nodded.

Their wedding planner and her assistant stepped forward to open the double doors to the church in unison.

"Wait," Hank said suddenly.

The ladies stepped back, letting the door stay closed.

Bianca turned and looked up at him. "Something wrong, Daddy?"

"I just want you to know how proud I am of you. How proud I have always been."

Bianca smiled and reached up to stroke his face, "I know that, Daddy."

"I think a lot about how my life would be if you hadn't forgiven me and come home. I'd probably have drunk myself to death and still been married to that barracuda."

Bianca nodded, knowing that he had taken Trishon and Papa Doc's betrayal hard—but never once had his sobriety wavered. Along with Dante, all three were serving time for their crimes and long gone from their lives.

"I really and truly want you to be happy because you deserve it, Bunny. I have my business back, and my daughter back, and I'm man enough to admit that I cannot thank you enough for that."

Bianca blinked away her tears, sniffing, as she smiled at him. "I think I know what this little talk is really about."

Hank looked bashful. "Oh you do?"

"You're not losing me again, Daddy. We'll still see each other everyday at the ranch, especially with my clinic set up there and anytime you need me, just call. Nothing or no one is coming between us again . . . okay?"

"Promise?"

"I promise."

Hank smiled, his grin almost as wide as his broad face. "Then let's get this thing rolling."

Bianca reached up on her toes to kiss both of his cheeks.

The planner and her assistant opened the doors.

Bianca took a deep breath as her father squeezed her hand comfortingly. Quickly she scanned the church, and saw many of her friends from Atlanta, including Armand, who pointed to Garcelle and then gave Bianca a wicked and mischievous smile. Bianca took in her soon to be in-laws, feeling love from them all. Mimi, serving as her bridesmaid, stood near the altar in her smart and sexy lavender suit. At the front of the church Kahron turned to watch her walk to him, looking handsome in his tuxedo. Bianca smiled with all the love she felt for him as she walked down the aisle into her destiny.

Dear Readers,

Heated was one of my favorite stories to write. A love scene that is one full chapter in length—I didn't realize that until I was done with it. Guess I got caught up—smile.

I hope you all enjoyed Kahron and Bianca's tale of love, passion, betrayal, and just a bit of suspense, as much as I enjoyed writing it. Of course, you probably caught all the hints that the next in what I am now naming the "Hot Holtsville Series" is Kade and Garcelle. Their story will be just as spicy, and romantic, and, I hope, as treasured as all the rest.

See you soon between the steamy pages of another story of what I like to call "Soul Love."

Love 2 Live & Live 2 Love.

And I'm out.

N.

Reading Group Guide Questions

1. The book opens with Bianca estranged from her father for well over a decade. Do you agree with her reasons for leaving home? Why? Would you have handled her issues with her father differently? Have you ever been in a situation you felt was best to leave?

2. When Bianca returned to Holtsville, she discovered how drastically Trishon had changed the family home. How would you deal with the same situation? Although she disliked Trishon and didn't approve of Trishon marrying her father, do you think Bianca handled the situation well?

3. With her father struggling to stay sober, do you think Bianca should have tried to convince Mimi to stop drinking as well? Was she being hypocritical? Do you expect more from your parents than you expect from your friends?

4. Do you think Kahron and Bianca's relationship became sexual too soon? Do any of you have a time frame on when you will allow sexual intimacy in new relationships? Would you have liked for your first time with a new lover to take place in a secluded spot in the woods like Bianca? Was the chemistry between Kahron and Bianca evident from the very beginning? What scene in the book showed that chemistry the best?

5. Did it take too long for Bianca to finally trust Kahron? Do you feel Kahron did enough to garner Bianca's trust? At anytime in the book did you feel Kahron might have

done the thing Hank accused him of? When? If so, when did you realize he wasn't involved?

6. Was Bianca foolish for running out to catch the "shadowy figure" in the yard, which led to her being knocked unconscious in the grove of trees? Have you ever played vigilante and regretted it? It was never revealed in the story, but who do you think was the second figure?

7. Do you think Kahron forgave Bianca too quickly during the scene on his porch? Was the scene believable? Why?

8. Trishon is a woman with some serious issues. Discuss her issues and how they relate to the crimes she committed. Are there any justifications in her actions? Are men as gullible as Trishon thinks? Do you think a woman like Trishon will ever be capable of falling in love?

9. What mistakes did Trishon, Dante, and Papa Doc make that led to their capture? Were you surprised to discover Papa Doc's involvement in Trishon's schemes?

10. Are you in love?

ABOUT THE AUTHOR

Niobia Bryant is the nationally bestselling and award-winning author of seven works of romance fiction. She lives in South Carolina with her boyfriend and is working on her next romance novel, *Count on This*, and her first mainstream novel, *Live and Learn*. For more on this author who cannot be stopped go to her Web site: *www.geocities.com/niobia_bryant*, where you can join her free online book club: Niobia Bryant News. Or feel free to email her at niobia_bryant@yahoo.com.

Grab These Other
Thought Provoking Books